THE VAMPIRE'S GAME

THE BLAIR GRAVES FILES
BOOK 3

MARNIE VINGE

For those of you who keep asking
will they or won't they?!

This one's for you.

CHAPTER ONE

"IT'S rude to invite yourself into someone else's house. Shoo," I say to the wolf spider about to make a break for it into my kitchen. I put my Doc Marten down in front of it and gently nudge it back out onto the patio. The wolf spider scurries, albeit ungratefully, back into the flower bed next to the back patio doors.

I glance at my watch. It's 7:15 in the evening and Cash is set to be here in about fifteen minutes. Food is in the oven, almost ready, and the wine is chilling.

We've seen each other on and off over the last few months, but he's been busy with family matters and I've been trying to find my place in the world now that the renovation of the Solomon House, now *chez* Graves, is complete. I'm getting restless and need to find something to do. Drinking too much and spending my dad's money just isn't hitting the spot like it used to.

Not that it ever *really* hit the spot.

There was always a gaping cavernous maw groaning for more no matter how much I put into it.

Things have been better lately, though.

Tonight's the first time I've seen Cash in over two months. He's had his head buried in whatever he's dealing with family-wise. I haven't pried, but I have a feeling it has to do with his dad. That situation can't be easy to navigate and I, of all people, should know how to give grace in such circumstances. So, that's what I try to do.

I'm looking forward to seeing him. Despite that, I'm anxious and I can't put my finger on *why*.

It's not like this is the first time I'm meeting him. And it's not like this is a date.

We never really talked about the almost kiss back in Hobby Hollow. We both left it alone, apparently afraid to touch it with a ten foot pole. I know my reasons, but I wonder about his.

Maybe it was something he looked at as a mistake. Or an almost mistake. Maybe he doesn't want to chance losing me as a friend, just like I don't want to chance that with him. Or maybe he doesn't really have any feelings for me beyond the platonic and that was a lapse in judgment brought on by too much time in each other's company in the middle of nowhere.

It's been enough to keep me up at night, so when he reached out and wanted to get together, I was receptive. Nervous, but receptive. And I don't know what I think is going to happen tonight to even be nervous about.

Maybe it's just seeing him after so much time. I do spend a lot of time alone in this house, which is another reason that I need to find something to do. Volunteer work or maybe a job. I'm not sure. I just know I'm tired of feeling lost and the most found I feel is when I'm with him.

Which is enough to make my cold, little, black heart want to crawl right out of my throat and vomit itself onto the tile below me with a wet *splat*.

Best not to think about that. At least for now.

I look at my watch again and only a minute has passed. I'm not the greatest cook in the world so we're having a casserole that I threw together from an easy recipes blog. I go to the fridge and check to see if the wine's cold yet, and it is. So, I pour myself a glass to dispel some of my jitters.

I take a long sip and check my phone. There's a text from Cash letting me know he's on his way. He left his house about five minutes ago so he should be here right on time. I have no other new notifications.

I raise my glass to my lips, but just before they meet, there's a pounding knock at the door. The kind of knock that's usually reserved for FBI raids.

"Coming!" I shout as the knocking persists.

I set my glass down and scurry up the hallway to the front door. I peer out the window and see that I know my guest, and she doesn't usually resort to such feral ways to announce her presence.

"Noelle," I say as I swing the door open.

She steps past me, a rush of air and a hint of cinnamon accompany her. She looks like a mess and she's talking about a mile a minute.

"They didn't think it was going to happen Friday, but it's happening! I don't know what to do. My family's gone insane. They want me to—"

"Slow down," I tell her as she paces the foyer. Her wild eyes meet mine and she looks like she's about to cry.

"I'm sorry," she says, slowing down only briefly. "I meant to say *hi* before I launched into it."

"What's going on?" I ask as I shut the door behind us, sealing out the chilly fall air.

"It's Jenna," Noelle says.

The name hangs there in the air between us for a moment, neither of us really wanting to touch it next. But I speak first.

"Is she—"

Noelle cuts me off, too eager to tell me.

"She's getting out of prison on Friday. I didn't expect it to happen like this," she says.

"Come on," I gesture for her to follow me back to the kitchen. I need my wine for this. "You want a drink?"

"Please, and make it a double," Noelle says.

She follows me and I pour her an extremely full glass of wine. I hand it to her and she takes a grateful and large first gulp. Then another. And a third. Then she sits it down on the counter and starts to talk again. I sip my wine and listen, doing the things that friends are meant to do sometimes: not offer advice, only a safe set of ears.

"It's just happening so quickly. And they want me to help organize a homecoming for her," Noelle says. She takes another long sip of wine after ranting for a second about her extended family. "Can you imagine? Asking *me* to help with this?"

"I can't believe they did that," I say.

Noelle testified against Jenna. Her testimony is part of what put her in prison.

"I can't either," Noelle says.

"Of all the obtuse things they could have done," I mutter, trying to wrap my mind around why her aunt would have thought this was a good idea.

"Apparently," she goes on. "Jenna and Uncle Joe made nice while she was in prison." Noelle rolls her eyes. I arch an eyebrow.

"Not very easy to make peace with the person you almost stabbed to death," I remark.

"My thoughts exactly," Noelle says.

I try to imagine what Jenna must have said—what verbal gymnastics she might have performed—to make *that* happen. I can't imagine making nice with the person that wanted me dead.

"And, to top it all off, she's going to be living with them," she adds.

"With your aunt and uncle?"

"Mommy and step-daddy dearest," Noelle says bitterly.

"And they want you to throw a homecoming party for her?" I ask.

"They think we can all just go back to being one big happy family," Noelle said. "I guess. When we weren't ever really one big happy family to begin with. Jenna always hated Joe."

I nod solemnly. It's an instance where I don't even know where to begin to try and make it better. I go back to my thought about just being a safe set of ears.

"Are you in the middle of something?" Noelle asks, noticing the two plates on the table and the casserole in the oven. "Oh, God. Are you having someone over? And I just showed up."

She sets her glass down on the counter and makes like she's going to leave.

"Stay," I tell her. "You're fine. It's just Cash," I say.

And, as if he's a devil that's been summoned, I hear him knock on my door.

CASH'S KNOCK is hardly as aggressive as Noelle's. He knocks thrice and waits patiently.

I swing the door open and he stands there wearing faded jeans that hug his thighs, a black leather jacket that looks like it's been well worn in, and a pair of black boots. His gray t-shirt peeks out from beneath the lapels of his jacket.

"Blair," he says, a wide grin spreading across his face, almost like he's not conscious of it. It makes me blush and I look away for a second.

"Hey," I manage.

He steps inside and wraps me in a huge bear hug and lifts me off the ground.

"It's been too long!" he says.

"It really has, hasn't it?" I ask when he puts me down.

He towers over me, a gentle giant, and I look up at him, wanting him to wrap me in another hug.

I bat away the thought.

"Come in," I say, gesturing to the hallway.

He steps inside and I close the door behind him.

"We've got company," I tell him quietly.

Just then, Noelle comes around the corner.

"Hi, Cash," she says. "Sorry to crash y'all's party," she adds with a sheepish smile.

"No worries," Cash says.

But he glances at me just then and there's a fleeting expression on his face. Almost like he wants to say he wishes it was just going to be the two of us.

You're imagining things, Blair.

He looks away and greets Noelle.

"Hi, Noelle. How are you?" he asks.

Noelle barks out a funny little laugh.

"Other than having to organize a party for the cousin I put in prison, I'm great," she says with a manic smile.

"That sounds...stressful," Cash says. "Wait a second," he adds. "That cousin wouldn't be Jenna Prescott would it?" he asks. Cash knows Noelle's last name and Cash knows a lot about true crime in the state of Oklahoma, particularly the kind of crime that haunts the Prescott family.

One that involves vampires.

CHAPTER TWO

CASH SITS and quietly listens to Noelle go over the finer details of things, the three of us gathered in the living room.

"I read a lot about the case when it was happening," Cash says to Noelle after she concludes her tale by telling Cash how her testimony was part of what put Jenna in prison. "I actually helped your dad with some research for the book he wrote about it."

My eyebrows shoot up. Now he's talking to me. And I know of no such book.

"My dad...wrote a book about this?" I ask.

The thought is absurd. Noelle's been my friend since she was a teenager. My dad would have mentioned this to me. He knew Noelle's last name. If he wrote a book about it, he would have put two and two together and been up my ass about talking to her.

Wouldn't he have?

A horrible thought comes to me. Maybe he wouldn't have. The idea of him just keeping everything to himself sends a shiver down my spine that has nothing to do with the supernatural and everything to do with a relationship that I'll never get a chance to repair.

Cash treads gingerly. He knows a little bit about the dynamics between my dad and I, and he used to work for him back when Cash was in college and I was a teenager.

Right around the time all of this happened. So that checks out.

" Cash says. "It's actually a book about the vampire subculture in America as a whole, but this case is what got him interested in it. And he followed the trail of a guy claiming to be a real vampire throughout the book."

I say nothing but feel sort of hollow.

I've been doing better lately with all the emotions surrounding my dad's disappearance and legal death. The new life that it bought me here at the Solomon House. But this feels like salt in a wound that's trying to heal. Just another reminder of how things were between us. I can look with rose tinted glasses all I want, but the fact remains that my dad and I were never close. He, Blake, and I were the opposite of a tight knit family.

I clear my throat and try to change the subject.

"So, what is Janelle wanting you to do?" I ask, referring to Jenna's mom, Noelle's aunt.

"Figure out the food. Figure out the decorations," Noelle says, swirling her wine in her glass. She takes another big drink. "Basically she wants me to make this into a party and it doesn't feel very much like an occasion for a party to me."

"Can you tell her you don't want to do it?" Cash asks.

"I wish," Noelle says. "My family would disown me. They expect me to bury the hatchet if Joe did. Janelle basically said as much when she talked to me on the phone," Noelle adds. "She told me 'let bygones be bygones and let's be a family again.' So, if I don't go, I'm the bad guy here even though Jenna was holding the knife."

"I'm familiar with toxic family dynamics," Cash says with a bitter smile.

We exchange a glance and for a second, I think he's seeking comfort from me. He offers me a sad smile. I return it, knowing just what he means about toxic family dynamics. It's been months since I've spoken to my twin, Blake. The last time I heard from him was when our dad's estate was settled after he was declared legally dead. Since then, nothing.

Cash reaches out a hand and squeezes my knee. I thrill at his touch, and I hate myself for it.

I blush and look away. His hand is gone just as quickly as it came.

"It sucks, right?" Noelle asks.

"It's never fun," Cash confirms with a mirthless laugh.

It makes me wonder just what's been going on with his dad recently. All the time that we didn't see each other, he kept saying that he was taking care of his dad. I wonder if he tried to get him to move back in with him. But if he did, likely it failed, and Norman's back out on the streets, homeless.

Cash has tried several times to get his dad out of the homeless shelter. Every time he's failed. They can't live together because Norman has a proclivity for street drugs and he's a raging alcoholic. Staying with Cash would mean getting off of those things. Getting off of those things would mean facing whatever demons he's battling, and he's just not ready to do that.

"I'm sorry I stayed so late," Noelle says, starting to get up from her seat. She finishes off the rest of her wine glass and marches it into the kitchen and returns. "I'll get out of your hair and you guys can eat, drink, and be merry. I'm sorry I crashed your date."

"Oh, it's not—" I say.

"That's alright—" Cash says.

And I notice that he didn't correct her. I clear my throat and silence myself.

I walk Noelle to the door. Cash hangs back in the living room.

"Noelle," I say as she hugs me on the porch. I pull

away and look at her. "Why don't you let me come with you on Friday? Be a buffer for you."

"You would do that?" Noelle's eyes look pleading, like she'd wanted to ask this all night.

"Of course, silly!" I tell her. "I don't mind at all. Jenna doesn't scare me." I laugh.

But something passes over Noelle's face that tells me Jenna *does* scare her.

And *that* scares me.

"I OFFERED TO GO WITH HER," I tell Cash as I round the corner back into the living room.

The fire is going, casting an orange glow out across the maximalist rug composed of an intricate jungle scene that sits beneath the furniture. Every time I look at it I think I find something new. I've spent the last few months really making this place my own.

"That was good of you. You're a good friend, Blair," Cash says.

He looks at me as he says the last and a sad smile crosses his lips again.

"You okay?" I ask.

I don't know how much I can pry without it being...well, *prying*. And I don't want to make him uncomfortable. But I would like to know what's going on with him.

"Yeah, I'm fine," he says. "Just had a lot going on. That's all."

I feel a stone drop in my gut. I don't want him to shut me out.

"I understand," I say. "Your dad?"

"Yeah," Cash says. "It's a long story and I'm sure you're not up for it tonight."

"I might surprise you," I say with a smile, but then I yawn as if on cue.

"Ah, see, I told you," he teases.

"We haven't even had dinner yet," I tell him. "I'm just an old lady these days."

"The time change will do that to you," he says.

We're making small talk and I don't like it. I go for it.

"Cash, what's going on with your dad?"

He sighs, rubs his face with both his hands, and speaks.

"My dad is a complicated guy," he says. "And things are just beginning to settle back down with him. I really would rather talk about anything else, Blair," he says. "Not because I don't want to discuss it with you, it's just all that I've discussed for the last several months and I'm exhausted."

I try not to be hurt by his words. But they sting anyway.

I want him to tell me everything. I only need to look in the mirror, though, to know what emotional unavailability looks like. My father taught me well. Cash isn't being emotionally unavailable, though. He just doesn't want to talk about it and that's more than fair.

I dust my emotional shoulders off and invite him to come get something to eat.

We both get out food and wine glasses and sit down at the table.

"So, I guess you know all the backstory on what's going on with Noelle," I say, changing the subject.

"I only know what was in your dad's book and what she told us just now," Cash said.

I nod. I decide to ask him about the book.

"This book my dad wrote," I say. "What can you tell me about it?"

"Well, this case—the Jenna Prescott case—prompted him to look into it all in the first place. As you know, there was a roleplaying game at the center of everything, with Jenna and her boyfriend, Peter, at the heart of it, leading the game."

I do know this. Noelle played the very game in question. It's something we rarely, if ever, speak of. It's just a game like Dungeons and Dragons, harmless. But Jenna turned it into something dark.

"Anyway, the game got out of hand, Jenna asked Peter to help her kill her stepfather, and you know the rest," Cash says.

Noelle was there when Jenna was going to go through with it. She witnessed Jenna stab Joe thirteen times. Miraculously, she missed any major arteries and Joe survived. Noelle's testimony put her away, or at least played a big part in the verdict and her sentencing. The court didn't really like that Jenna had been manipulating a young girl. Peter called the cops on Jenna when she told him what she was going to do, taking off in her car with Noelle in tow. That was probably what ultimately saved Joe's life. The EMTs were there within a minute of the stabbing.

That night changed Noelle's life. And the lives of everyone involved.

I met Noelle shortly after that, at the beginning of high school. She had transferred from her previous school, garnering far too much unwanted attention from classmates. I was a bit of a loner myself, so Noelle and I fit together like two puzzle pieces that had been looking for one another.

"The real mystery about the whole thing was why Jenna did it in the first place," Cash says.

"No one really had any idea," I reply. "Aside from her just hating her stepfather. I guess that's reason enough."

Cash makes a non-committal noise and I take a bite of my food.

"Anyway, back to the book," Cash says after taking a bite of his own food. "Your dad started doing a lot of research into these communities that claim to be vampiric. Some of them just play the roleplaying game and leave it at that. Others make it their whole lifestyle and even consume real, human blood. From willing donors, of course. Or at least they're willing in most cases. He covered some other vampire-related crimes. And in the process of doing the research for the book, he came across one very interesting source," Cash says.

I listen with rapt attention because this is a story I've never heard before. And it feels strange hearing it out of Cash's mouth and not my father's. But I want to know the rest and forget about the weirdness of the telling for a minute.

"The guy first contacted him via e-mail and they began a correspondence. The guy told him he was a *real* vampire and had lived for hundreds of years. Your dad did his best to track him down and came up empty handed at every turn. The guy knew a lot about the Jenna Prescott case and seemed to be quite fascinated with it."

"Well, that's creepier than hell," I tell Cash.

I try to imagine my dad, sitting down at his desk while Blake and I watched television in the other room, only for him to be reading letters from what sounds like a maniac. A real one.

"I'll say," Cash says. "The guy gave him a name and everything. Do you have any of your dad's old files?"

"I have a ton of them," I say. "Everything from the radio station is upstairs. I had to buy more filing cabinets to put it all away. I haven't gone through it, though."

"I wouldn't mind to help you," Cash offers. "I'd like

to look through some of that stuff, if it'd be alright with you, Blair."

"I don't mind at all," I tell him.

We eat the rest of our meal, making chit chat about what each of us has been up to, with Cash talking about everything that's kept him busy outside of taking care of his father. I tell Cash that I've spent a lot of time with Noelle and her boyfriend, Hooper, an old friend of ours from high school. I tell him that I'm glad Noelle has him.

After we finish eating, the pair of us sit, sipping our wine. Then Cash speaks.

"Blair, I have a proposition for you," he says.

I raise an eyebrow, never sure how these things are going to go with Cash. The last time he had a proposition for me, I ended up at a Bigfoot festival in the middle of a missing person investigation.

"What would that be?" I ask.

"Don't worry. It's nothing crazy," he says with a laugh. "I was wondering if you might want to, I don't know, help me with some stuff. Like research and production and all that," he says. And then after a beat he adds, "Permanently."

"You want to hire me as your assistant?" I ask, clarifying.

"Well, assistant isn't exactly the title I was thinking of. More like Chief Executive Ghost Procurer," he says. "Or something along those lines."

I laugh, then think about how I've been looking for

something that would keep me busy. And what would be better than this? An errant thought strays into my mind, telling me how much time I'd get to spend with Cash. I swipe it away like an annoying mosquito on a summer night.

"I'd be delighted to," I tell him.

He raises his glass to me, and we toast.

"To new beginnings," he says. "And to you finally getting a job."

"He's got jokes, ladies and gentlemen, and I have a sinking feeling that he'll be here all week," I tease back.

Cash laughs and I find myself sucked into the warmth of his smile.

CHAPTER THREE

I GET ready late Friday afternoon and take my time with a bath. I fill the claw-foot tub and get some bubbles going, then climb in and lean back, closing my eyes. Something about a bath seemed more appealing as the weather gets colder and chillier outside. The water steams, fogging up the mirror and the bubbles cover me completely. I slip in up to my nose and stay there for a moment, thinking about the evening that lies out in front of me.

I think about how Noelle looked at me when she left a few nights ago. The fear in her eyes. Noelle isn't someone that I think of as being scared of her own shadow. No, this was bigger than a shadow. This was something else entirely. She was scared of Jenna. And Jenna is very, very real.

That still alarms me.

My plan for the night is to be the best moral support I can be for Noelle and possibly run interference if I need to. I'm wary of Jenna, and the situation is concerning, but I refuse to be afraid of her.

Especially when Noelle needs me.

I soak for a good twenty minutes and then get out, dry off, and start fixing my hair.

Once I'm ready, I wait by the front door for Noelle to show up. And right when she said she'd be there, I see her headlights turn into my long driveway. She pulls into the circle in front of the house and rolls her window down just as I'm locking the door behind me.

"Your chariot awaits, madam!" Noelle calls out to me.

I laugh and bounce down the steps and over to the car. I climb in and off we go.

Noelle chatters as we drive and I barely get a word in. Finally, she pauses for just a moment. I seize the opportunity.

"Are you nervous?" I ask, even though the answer is obvious.

"No, no," Noelle says with a smile that's a little too bright.

"It's okay if you are, Noelle," I tell her. "This is a big deal. Feel your feelings."

"That's funny, coming from you, Miss Ice Box," she remarks with a laugh.

"This isn't about me," I tease her. "I'll feel my feelings when I'm good and ready, but you need to work through yours properly. Do as I say and not as I do," I add with a smile. I reach out and squeeze her arm.

She looks over at me, gratitude on her features.

"It's going to be alright," I reassure her.

She nods, hopefully taking what I'm telling her to heart.

Finally, Noelle makes the turn into Jenna's old neighborhood.

"Still rich, you see," Noelle says with half a laugh.

The neighborhood is old money. Jenna's stepfather came from money and got them a house in this historic section of the city. The houses have columns and look like something out of the nineteenth century. Older than my home. We pull up outside a house with two massive stone lions guarding the driveway like sentinels. The drive is a half-circle, and Noelle pulls right up in the middle and kills the engine. I look up at the house.

It stretches three stories with balconies on the second and third floors that look out across the street before the house. It's white stone and looks old but also kept up with. The flowerbeds are manicured perfectly and there are expensive-looking fall decorations on the porch. The kind of stuff you'd never find at a big box store. This stuff is crafted by artisans, likely purchased online or at a little boutique.

We get out of the car and Noelle walks around to

where I'm standing. Just then, I catch movement out of the corner of my eye at the front door. I look and see a woman in a white blouse and white pants waving at us with a smile on her face.

Janelle.

I wave and smile at her. She opens the glass door and calls out to us.

"You girls come on in!" she says with a bright smile.

I glance at Noelle, who has a fake grin plastered on her face. She almost looks like she might cry if given half a chance. I reach out and grab her by the hand. I squeeze. She looks over at me as if jarred out of a daydream. She smiles and squeezes back. Then she lets go of my hand and starts walking up the steps to the porch.

"You look lovely, Noelle," Janelle says in a sing song voice that I have a feeling she reserves for social occasions. For some reason, I can't imagine her being this nice to Noelle in private. It makes me glad I came. "And you, Blair," she says to me. But there's something about the pitch of her voice that rings false. It seems strained.

It makes me wonder how much she really wants to go through with this dinner.

"Follow me," Janelle says as we pass through the front door and into the house.

It swallows us up, this white mansion, and I have no idea what awaits us at the dinner table.

. . .

WE'RE the first ones here. Joe and Jenna went to run an errand and Noelle's sister and niece haven't arrived yet. From what I understand, that's the extent of the guest list tonight.

Noelle fiddles with the napkin in front of her. She rearranges her silverware several times, straightening it periodically, even though I'm not sure it can get much straighter. Janelle sits opposite us at the table and classical music plays low in the background.

I try to take control of the conversation, turning it to innocuous topics like Janelle's and Joe's jobs, asking them how they're doing. I leave out any mention of Jenna. I highlight some of Noelle's accomplishments in the last year, and she smiles briefly when I do. I do my best, but the fact remains that we're all here because Jenna's coming home. It's like it hangs in the air around us, thick enough to cut with a knife.

It makes me think maybe things aren't all sunshine and roses. Maybe there's trouble in paradise with the recent reconciliation between Jenna and Joe.

"How are you, Blair?" Janelle asks me.

I talk as long as I can, trying to ease Noelle's struggle. She hasn't said a word and I can tell she's nervous, getting more anxious by the minute. She keeps looking at the clock on the far wall of the formal dining room. But finally, we have to wait no more.

The front door opens.

The three of us look up and go silent.

Janelle excuses herself.

"That might be them now," she says with a smile.

But when she gets into the hallway, I hear a voice I recognize. Noelle visibly slumps back in her chair. The voice belongs to her sister, Nori.

I sigh.

"Well, that was anticlimactic," I say.

"You're telling me," Noelle whispers.

Nori comes around the corner into the formal dining room.

"Hi, Blair!" she says with a big smile. I haven't seen Nori in ages.

In tow is her teenage daughter, Mel. Melanie is fifteen and looks the part, earbuds shoved deeply into her ears and a look on her face that says she'd rather be anywhere but here. I smile understandingly at her and she offers me a quick, pressed smile that looks like it pains her to express.

The thought makes me laugh inwardly, remembering what Noelle and I were like when we were teenagers. And then that makes me think that I never knew Noelle before all of this happened. We met afterwards. After she changed schools. It wasn't long into our friendship that she told me everything.

I'm brought back to the idea that my dad wrote a whole book about this case and never once anything to me about it. Was he really that isolated in his own little world? Were we really that separated from each other?

I shrug it off. A thought for another time. Right

now, it might drag me down like an anchor falling into the deepest part of the sea. I need to be weightless, ready for quick-witted conversation. Not mired in my own past.

"How are you?" Nori asks Noelle. "Things going well with that new boyfriend of yours?"

"Things are fine," Noelle says with a smile but her tone is clipped.

Nori was always the fair-haired child. Noelle was the one that got into trouble. They were glad when she became friends with me because it stopped. We mostly kept to ourselves. The *trouble* that Noelle got into had everything to do with Jenna influencing her. Once that was removed, Noelle wasn't in trouble anymore. I want to tell them it's not rocket science, that Noelle was never the problem.

But I might be biting off more than I can chew if I start there.

And it might be counterproductive. I'm here to offer support, not make things worse.

"We're glad you girls could come," Janelle says to Nori and Mel, then she smiles at Noelle and me. "Especially you, Noelle. We're hoping that bygones can be bygones, hmm?"

The *hmm* doesn't invite debate or conversation. It's clear that Janelle is telling Noelle not to make problems tonight. I bristle at the implication.

Janelle seems to read it on my face. Her smile falters for only a moment.

They all make small talk, Noelle seemingly more at ease once the focus shifts to Mel and what she's been up to. I start to question the wisdom of bringing her to something like this when Noelle and I get a moment alone and she whispers to me.

"Nori wouldn't have brought Mel but she didn't have another choice," she says softly. Everyone else is busy in the kitchen, refreshing drinks and talking, which gives us a minute. It gives Noelle the chance to breathe.

"I was trying to imagine what had possessed her," I tell Noelle.

"I don't blame you," Noelle says. "I would have been thinking the same thing. A prison homecoming probably isn't the best place for a teenage girl, but welcome to my family." She offers me a lop-sided smile. It gets a grin out of me.

Noelle and I bonded over our equally dysfunctional families back when we first met. I told her that my dad chased ghosts on the radio and she told me she'd put her cousin in prison. It wasn't until a few months into our friendship that she divulged all the details. But seeing as how I wasn't exactly the most popular kid in school, I wasn't clamoring for them or pressuring her to share anything she wasn't ready to. I was just glad to have a friend.

Maybe that's one of the reasons I'm so protective over Noelle. Right now, all I can think is that I want to keep Jenna from hurting her. I have to fight the urge to talk back to Janelle any time she gets prickly with her. I can only imagine how much of myself I'll need to swallow once the lady of the hour gets here.

But I don't have to wait much longer, because just as the thought is occurring to me, there's a sound at the garage door that leads into the house. Two people talking. A man and a woman.

Joe and Jenna.

They're laughing. Noelle and I look at each other, unsure of what we're hearing. I arch an eyebrow and Noelle's eyes go wide, almost like a panicked animal. Like at any moment, she might decide to bolt. And I could hardly blame her. This is the last place I'd want to be given the circumstances. I'm still in shock that Janelle ever thought it was a good idea to put Noelle in this position to begin with.

People will do strange things to keep family secrets buried, though.

Very strange things.

"There you are!" I hear Janelle making over Jenna in the hallway. She greets Nori and Mel. I hear Joe talking to all of them. And beside me, I can feel Noelle's body stiffen.

"It's going to be okay," I tell her.

She reaches for my hand under the table and squeezes. She nods without looking at me. Her eyes remain glued on the doorway that leads from the hall into the dining room.

And then, like some dark angel, Jenna appears.

Her hair is a dish-water blonde. Not like the raven black I remember from pictures. And she wears a white t-shirt and jeans. She's not decked out in the goth ensemble that made the front page of the papers. Her face isn't made up and she looks almost normal. But still, there's something ethereal about her. Other-worldly. And she lays eyes on Noelle the moment she steps into the room.

I brace myself for Noelle to fall apart, but that's not what happens.

What happens is strange.

Jenna stares at her for a moment and then her mouth cracks into a smile. Her hand goes to her mouth and tears fill her eyes. Before I know what to say or do, Noelle is standing up from the table and heading over, wrapping Jenna in a long hug. They sway, both of them laughing, Noelle beginning to cry, too.

I feel like I've stepped into the *Twilight Zone*.

I smile nervously at Janelle, who looks on from the doorway, seemingly very happy with this turn of events.

"You look beautiful," Jenna says when she breaks away from Noelle's embrace.

"You do, too," Noelle says with a laugh.

All the tension from the last half hour has melted away and I'm left in its wake feeling like I have no idea what the hell is going on. I've never seen a shift like this happen so quickly. I was never in Jenna's presence as a teenager and it's hard to know what's going on inside Noelle's head, but I can't help but worry that it might be easy for her to fall back under Jenna's sway.

Everyone takes a seat and we have dinner. Jenna regales us with charming tales of prison life and Joe and Janelle laugh. Noelle's focus is solely on Jenna. A few times I try to get her attention, but to no avail. She's glued to her cousin and her animated features.

Jenna is charming, no doubt. And she has a charisma about her. She turns every story into an event and everyone is laughing, smiling, and enraptured by her presence.

I have no doubt she had no trouble making a place for herself in her cell block.

Knowing what I do about her, I imagine she got a lot of other people to do her dirty work for her. That seems to be her *modus operandi*.

Joe refills our glasses and we eat the dessert that came with the Mexican food Noelle made sure was delivered before we got here. Jenna holds court and I watch suspiciously, weighing her every movement.

Finally, her focus turns to matters closer to home.

"I'm so glad you came, Noelle," she says. "I was afraid you might not."

"I wouldn't have missed it," Noelle says with a smile.

And I want to slap her into next week. That's

hardly what she was saying in the car ride on the way over here. She wanted to be practically *anywhere* else.

Jenna may never have been a real vampire, but I can certainly see the affinity she felt for the creature. By the time dinner is over, I feel drained, and Noelle looks like a version of herself that I've never seen.

I don't like it one bit.

CHAPTER FOUR

AFTER EVERYONE FINISHES EATING, I excuse myself to go to the bathroom. It's all I can do to keep my skin from crawling right off my body. I step into the hall and for the first time all evening, I take a deep breath. I sigh as I step into the hall bathroom, and I lock the door behind me. I sit there longer than I need to, just trying to give myself a breather. Jenna's presence is suffocating.

Even as an outsider, I can feel the hold she has on everyone. Even after all this time. I half expected her to be this watered-down version of herself, but that wasn't the case. There's something about her that I can't quite put my finger on, but it reminds me of every documentary I've ever seen about Jim Jones.

The charisma, I guess.

It's the same kind of charisma that's usually reserved for cult leaders and handsome serial killers.

Whatever it is, she's got it.

I grab my phone out of my pocket after I wash my hands, and I shoot a text to Cash.

> This is beyond weird

I don't have to wait long before the little bubble pops up to let me know he's typing out a reply.

> I want to see you later. Can I come over? Also can't wait to hear about it.

I tell him *sure* and leave it at that. I'm sure he'll want a run down on what it was like to be in Jenna's presence, especially since he knows the finer details of the case, apparently. It strikes me then how the person I want to talk to about all of this is him.

I'm stressed and I want to turn to him.

I wonder if he felt the same way when he was dealing with everything with his dad. I think about how some nights, during the last few months, he'd randomly text me at two or three in the morning. Nothing too telling, but maybe a link to an article that made him think of me or a question about something. Almost like he was reaching out, needing contact. Needing reassurance, maybe.

That's how I'm feeling right now. And the person I want it from is him.

I realize that's a dangerous place to be at in my head and in my heart.

I tell myself that my heart rate picking up when I read his words has nothing to do with him and everything to do with the stressful situation I'm in. Forget that it didn't happen until the moment I saw his text. That's irrelevant, right?

That's what I'm telling myself.

I tuck my phone into my back pocket and grab the doorknob, twist, and pull. I step out into the hallway and almost instantly, I run into someone in the darkness.

"Oh!" I say. "Sorry!"

"No worries," I hear Jenna say.

I make out her form in the shadowy hallway. Her hair hangs long on either side of her face, framing it well. It should be criminal to get out of prison and look as good as she does. It hasn't touched her when it comes to aging.

The darkness seems to take to her. Like she's one with it. Like she knows how to control it. She flashes me a smile that catches what little light there is in here and her teeth glint for half a second.

"I've heard a lot about you, Blair," she says.

Her voice comes out almost like the purring of a cat. There's something calculated about her words. And I don't like it.

"Good to know," I say. "I've heard a lot about you, too, Jenna," I say evenly, intent on holding my ground with her. The last thing I want her to know is how uneasy she makes me. She reminds me of a shark, and as such, she might smell blood in the water if she gets an inkling of how uncomfortable I am right now.

I don't want to be in the hallway alone with her. Not in the same house where she almost killed Joe.

It's too weird. And I feel too vulnerable.

She stands there for a moment, not saying anything, just taking me in. I feel like she's weighing me, sizing me up for something. Her eyes travel down my body, feeling like little hands, examining every inch of me. My skin crawls under her gaze the same way it has in the past with other predators.

I swallow, suddenly feeling conscious of everything about myself. My mouth is dry and I struggle to speak.

"I'll just excuse myself," I say.

The words come out softer and far meeker than I mean for them to.

And I swear there's something satisfied in Jenna's expression. Even in the shadows, I can see it. I can feel it. Her energy is tangible, a serpent coiling around us. And I long to be back in the presence of everyone else.

I side step her and the spell is broken. I cast a look over my shoulder just in time to see the bathroom door close. I shiver and step back into the dining room where I take my seat next to Noelle.

"I think we're about ready to head out," Nori says.

Noelle nods her head and Janelle thanks us all for being there.

The group of us get our things and meander out onto the front porch. I'm thankful for the fact that

Jenna's still in the bathroom, though part of me wonders what's taking her so long.

"We're so glad that you could join us," Janelle says to Noelle.

Noelle hugs Janelle and I cringe. Something is off.

Just then, Jenna steps out onto the porch with the rest of us. There's something weird about seeing her out here in the open. Like she should be somewhere else—somewhere confined.

Like prison.

Or maybe even in a coffin.

She steps forward and wordlessly wraps Noelle in an embrace. Noelle squeezes her back and Jenna cups the back of her head. It would be tender if I had no knowledge of the history between the two of them. As it is, it sets my teeth on edge.

I fold my arms over my chest, wanting as much between me and Jenna as possible. I want that for Noelle, too.

Dread knots in my gut as we say our goodbyes and I climb into the passenger seat of Noelle's car. She gets in and closes her door. The cab is quiet. Awkwardly so. I can already feel a curtain descending between the two of us. Two different versions of events tonight are circulating in both our minds and I feel scared for Noelle.

"Well, that went way better than I expected," Noelle says as we turn out of the neighborhood.

I don't say anything. I'm not sure *what* to say, but I

know I need to say *something*. My silence is going to give me away and I'm afraid it's already done that by the time I speak.

"I'm glad," I say.

My tone doesn't match my words, though. It's like a smile that doesn't quite reach the eyes.

And Noelle picks up on it.

"Are you okay?" she asks.

"I'm fine," I say a little too quickly. "Are you okay?" That's the real question.

"I'm good," Noelle says. "You know, I didn't expect that she would have changed, but she seems like she has," she goes on. "I never thought I'd say that. Honestly," she laughs.

"It takes a lot for a person to actually change," I say cautiously.

Noelle seems to bristle at that.

"She's done the work, Blair," she says. "You heard her."

She's referencing the stories that Jenna told us about finding spirituality in prison. I look out the passenger side window and roll my eyes. I want to shake Noelle.

"Just be careful," I tell her.

"It's not like I'm friends with her," Noelle says sharply.

So, I say nothing else on the way home.

· · ·

BY THE TIME Cash shows up, I've had two glasses of wine, and I've worked myself up into a real frenzy. I'm annoyed at Noelle, thinking that she's going to get involved with Jenna again and worrying myself sick about it. Finally, Cash knocks at the door.

"Coming!" I call. I was already pacing the hall before he got here.

I throw the door wide and gesture for him to come in.

"I see you've started without me. That bad, huh?" Cash glances at my wine glass.

"It was pretty bad, if I'm being honest," I tell him. "You wouldn't believe her. The way she just had them all wrapped around her finger. It was weird as fuck."

"People who get other people involved in attempted homicide typically have that trait," Cash says somewhat sarcastically. I stick my tongue out at him.

"Do you want some?" I point at the wine. He nods.

I go back to the kitchen and pour him a glass, then we head for the living room.

"I'm just worried about Noelle," I tell him. It's the truth. "I didn't like the way she looked at Noelle," I tell him. "Like a meal or something. She looked at me the same way, but my judgment wasn't clouded with history."

Cash nods solemnly.

"It tracks with everything your dad said about the

case. He never actually interviewed Jenna, but he interviewed her ex-boyfriend, Peter," he says.

"And what did he have to say about the Queen of the Night?" I ask, my tone dripping with venom.

I'm not protective over many things, but the two things that I am are my memories of my father and my best friend.

"He was affected by the whole thing. Jenna was everything to him. Turning her in to the cops really did a number on him," Cash says. "He was broken when your dad interviewed him. Still in love with her, too."

"I can certainly imagine that," I tell him.

And I can. With the way everyone acted about her tonight, I wouldn't be surprised if there was a line of guys out there who were still in love with Jenna Prescott. What concerns me the most, though, is the rose-colored glasses that Noelle seems to be looking at her with.

"I don't know what it is," I tell him. "I think maybe it's some kind of approval thing for Noelle. It was like as soon as she laid eyes on Jenna, she was a kid again, seeking her approval."

"That would make sense," Cash says. "That happened at a critically formative time in her life. I can certainly understand if there's a part of her that still longs for Jenna's approval. Especially since she helped to put her away for so long."

I nod. It makes sense. I don't like it, but it tracks.

"She's never so much as mentioned that to me,

though," I say, fighting with the idea. "I've thought for years that Noelle was past it."

"People have a funny way of silently and expertly carrying their wounds around with them," Cash says, giving me a pointed look.

"I'm not interested in a psychoanalysis session," I tell him shortly.

He holds up both hands, but he smirks, clearly pleased that he hit a nerve.

There's a degree of comfort it in, even though it annoys me. Cash knows me. At least as well as I let anyone know me. The only person that knows me better is probably Noelle.

"I'm just worried about her," my tone softening. "I just don't want her to get involved with Jenna again. I can't imagine that going anywhere good."

"You can't keep her from it," Cash says. "She's a grown woman. She'll do what she's going to do," he adds. "But I understand the impulse."

"It's hard when you can't get the people you love to do what they should," I say with a bitter smile.

Cash echoes that smile on his own face. He takes a long sip of his wine.

"Indeed," he says, looking into the glass.

It brings my thoughts back to his dad.

It also makes me wonder what I don't know about Cash and think about what he still doesn't know about me.

We only let people see the parts of us that we want to.

It occurs to me then that I wish I could let Cash know me entirely. Really know me. All of me. And that I want the same from him. Sitting here with him in silence, the thought saddens me. I'm not sure that's something that's in the cards for us.

"I wanted to talk to you about something," Cash says finally.

"What's up?" I ask.

"You know how I asked you to help me with some stuff? Well, I think I have your first assignment," he says.

I sit up straighter in my seat. This is what I've needed. A project. Or something like one.

"The whole Jenna thing has my mind on vampires," he says. "And I've been thinking about that vampire that your dad tried to track down. I want to look into that. And do a whole series of videos on vampires. All the aspects. Folklore, true crime, all of it. And I need your help," he says.

"I could probably clear some time in my schedule for that," I tell him with a smirk.

He smiles back at me and the smile touches all of his features. Sometimes I don't realize how handsome he is. He takes a sip of wine and looks at me over the rim of the glass.

"I'm glad that you can find some time for it," he says with a smile.

"I do what I can for people I like," I tell him. And I smile back.

CHAPTER FIVE

I BURY myself in the research for Cash's latest project.

I didn't expect to take to it like I have, but it's been thoroughly enjoyable. Usually, the word research would make me think of college essays about obscure pieces of literature and MLA formatting, but this is entirely different. This is actually *fun*.

It's not something I would have admitted only a year ago. The idea that any of this could be worthwhile. But now, I'm looking at it with a different perspective. My hard edge toward my dad has softened somewhat, and I see the value in what Cash does. At least most of the time these days.

There's still a part of me that wonders if any of this is real, despite how *very* real my own experiences have been. I can still talk myself out of them given enough free room to move in my mind.

It would be easier that way, wouldn't it? If none of this was real.

Certainly, more convenient.

I hadn't counted on getting into my thirties and experiencing a paradigm shift.

However, I'm skeptical about the vampire thing. Ghosts are one thing and Bigfoot is another, but vampires surely even stretch Cash's ability to suspend disbelief. Or at least that's what I'm telling myself as I embark on this research.

The first cursory searches I do between the web and the library's resources turn up links to Wikipedia articles about vampires. Both those from folklore and myth and those from true crime. I hit on a couple of serial killers but decide to save that reading for later. Right now, all I'm interested in is an overview.

I stumble onto an academic page with some good info. I begin to read.

Vampires have long been a source of fascination and fear for humans. The earliest incarnations of the creature date back long before Christ walked the earth. From the Greek lamiae to the Chinese Jiāng Shí, there is some incarnation of the blood-sucking fiend in just about every culture. So, what is it about vampires that has captured our imagination so thoroughly? Is it the idea that it could be anyone we know, risen from the grave, come back to slake their bloodthirst? Or is it the very idea that our blood is some sort of magical elixir, capable of keeping the undead *alive* long after their heart stops beating? The vampire has transcended time and, every so often, reinvents itself. From the beast of yore to the romantic, seductive vampire of today, the creature has long been with us and will long *be* with us, if the past is any predictor.

I go on to read the full article, which gives a broad overview of the vampire subject ranging from Greek mythology all the way up to modern vampire novels and films. It seems that the creature isn't going anywhere, regardless of how real or fake it might be. Something catches my eye toward the end of the article. A bit about vampire roleplaying.

There have been many games in later years that involve players assuming the role of the vampire. Some of these games have gotten out of hand, such as in the case of Jenna Prescott. It seems that in these cases, the lure of the undead and the idea of the power that they might possess proved to be fatal for some.

Wow. Jenna was mentioned on a university website in an article about vampires. Jesus.

That's some sort of distinction, I guess.

I bite back my irritation. I think about the way that Noelle looked at her. How it was like Jenna cast a spell as soon as she walked into the room. It was like some unearthly incantation was cast as soon as words passed out of her lips. Somehow, I remained immune from it. Maybe it was just the fact that I don't share a history with Jenna. Maybe she wasn't aiming it at me. Whatever it was, I'm glad.

Grateful, even.

And it strikes me then how much like a vampire she is. The way that she can *glamour* people and put them under her spell. She draws them into her game and makes their will her own. It's frightening to think about.

I imagine Noelle, a teenager, listening to everything Jenna had to say. Playing that stupid game, pretending they were vampires. I imagine how things might have gone entirely differently. How bad that whole situation could have been for Noelle if one or two events were changed slightly.

I might never have met her.

She might be in prison now.

And Joe might really be dead.

I can't believe I sat across the table from an attempted murderer.

And that her would be victim carried on with her all night as if nothing ever happened.

The whole thing is too weird and makes me wonder what else I don't know about Noelle's family.

Everyone has their secrets, and families will guard those at all costs. My dad didn't even have any big secrets—or at least none that I know of—and he guarded his private life with everything he had.

Imagine if he'd really been trying to conceal something.

The thought is chilling, and it makes me reach for the blanket sitting on the couch next to me. I wrap it around my shoulders, which suddenly feel too bare and exposed, even here in my own home.

I glance over at the fire blazing in the hearth. It casts an orange and yellow light across the living room, across my jungle rug. I look down at it. At the predators and prey engaged in an eternal dance in the tapestry of it all. I think about Jenna, whom I believe to be the ultimate predator.

And then I think of Noelle.

Someone whom I've always thought was the ultimate prey.

It makes sense that Jenna would want her back under her sway.

I know that I meant to be looking up things about the basics on vampires, but now I want to look into the roleplaying games. It's like a splinter that just slipped under my skin, worrying at my flesh and impossible to be ignored until I remove it at the root.

I do a quick search and immediately several games pop up. I scroll through them all and find one for sale on eBay that catches my eye.

It's Vampires: the Hunted and the year on this particular game is 1999.

The art is standard for 80s and 90s horror novels and games. Which is to say that it's fantastically engaging. On the cover of the large manual is a vampire with a glass of what appears to be either dark red wine or blood in her hand. She wears a long, black dress a la Elvira or Morticia Addams. At her feet are two wolves that look like they're about to rip each other's throats out for a chance to lap up whatever might be left when she finishes drinking her fill.

Immediately, I'm struck by her resemblance to Jenna. Or at least the way Jenna looked in all the newspapers that covered the attempted murder. Pale skin, long flowing black hair, makeup contour so sharp that someone could cut themselves on it.

It's listed for $250. Apparently, it's out of print and this is a special edition. Something that a collector might be interested in. My finger hovers over the *Buy Now* button and I'm tempted. But $250 is an absurd amount to spend on a game for research. And I'm not even sure it would be research so much as satisfying my own curiosity.

Noelle has never really told me anything about the inner workings of the game she played with Jenna. And there's a part of me that wants to know. I resist the urge to make a ridiculous impulse purchase and navigate back to the search engine.

I gather some more sources. The first video in the series is going to be about the origins of the vampire myth. I organize my research, creating a new folder on my desktop for all of this. I pause for a moment and smirk, imagining my dad watching me now. Imagining how he'd probably get a kick out of the idea that I'm sort of following in his footsteps.

Especially since I spent such a long time, trying to make sure that would never happen. That thought makes my smile falter, bringing me back to the reality of what our relationship was.

And the fact that it's highly likely Cash knew my dad better than I ever did. It's a strange thought. One that never ceases to baffle me.

I wonder if I had kids right now, if I'd be better or if I'd fall victim to the Graves generational curse and shut my kids out of my life. Keep them separated from myself. I'd like to think I wouldn't.

That makes me think of Cash talking about my dad's book. The one about vampires. I close my laptop and get up from the living room. I head upstairs, taking them two at a time and rounding the corner into the bedroom that has served as a holding space for all his stuff.

I walk in and walk over to the bookshelf. I deposited all of his books here after I got the courage to go through most of his office paraphernalia. There are a number of strange volumes in his library and I spot the book I'm seeking almost instantly.

It's dusty on the top. Even though I've only been here for a year, I hardly touch my father's belongings. Even to dust. There's something about this room that reminds me of a museum. Like maybe I should leave the things inside of it alone.

I pluck the book off the shelf and walk out of the room, taking it back downstairs with me. I curl up again on the couch and look at the cover.

There's a man in a trench coat, walking away from

the camera. You can only see the lower half of his body. He casts a long shadow against a brick wall and the entire photo has been edited to appear red. A street-lamp glows in the distance on an empty street.

This copy has a pristine spine. It looks like it's never even been cracked open. I wonder if it was a copy given to him by the publisher back in the day. I thumb through it. It's thick and in the center is a collection of photographs. I glance at the first photograph. It's Jenna.

In the picture, Jenna is being walked by a police officer out of the courtroom immediately after being found guilty of attempted murder. She looks at the camera and sticks her tongue out, one eye closed in an expression that looks like it belongs on a girl's face in a spring break selfie. She's glib, nonchalant, like this is just an ordinary day for her. Like there's nothing terrifying about the fact that she's going to prison for a very, very long time.

It's startling. What's even more unsettling about it is thinking about how Noelle was with her the other night. How it seems like there's some kind of disconnect in her mind when it comes to Jenna. It's something I was never aware of until now, I think.

I flip the book over and look at the back. I read the description.

Vampires have lurked at the edges of society since its dawn. The revenant has plagued the nightmares of each society in its different forms over the centuries. In recent years, the vampire has infected pop culture and taken over at the movie theaters and the bookstores. With that has come a rise in self-identified vampires. America's vampire subculture has grown over the last decade. Join Graham Graves on a quest to uncover one of folklore's most beloved monsters as he ventures deep into this mysterious underground community.

On the back, below the description, is a picture of my dad.

In it, he wears a turtleneck and a blazer. He's leaning against a brick wall, not unlike the one on the cover. He looks serious. Like an authority on the topic. Which I guess he was. The thought makes me smile.

I run my thumb over the picture, wondering what happened to him.

But that's a question for another night. Tonight, I need to work on this episode outline.

So, I dive into the book and begin reading.

THE BEAUTIFUL AND THE DEAD
FOREWORD

The case that led me to write this book happened just down the road from where I live with my family. Perhaps *down the road* is an exaggeration, but Oklahoma City is a sprawling place. When my daughter was fourteen years old, the Prescott case broke.

That was the case that set me on this path. I became fascinated with the idea of a vampire subculture. Kids as young as mine were getting involved in the lifestyle thanks to games like Vampires: the Hunted. A big misconception arose about the people that play these games with shows like *60 Minutes* assuming they were all serial killers in the making.

The majority of people who love the vampire image identify themselves as nerds. Anne Rice's books made the vampire popular once more in the 1970s and then again in the 1990s when the book was adapted into the excellent film starring Brad Pitt and Tom Cruise.

In this book, I wanted to not only share my research on the topic, but present you with my own story to add to the collective vampire narrative.

In my research, I met someone—or almost met someone—who claimed to be a vampire. This person remained just outside of my reach for the entirety of the writing of this book, popping up here and there, leaving bread crumbs for me to follow.

I wanted to share that story with you.

In my research, I've found that ninety-nine percent of people who identify with vampires are harmless.

But that one percent...

That's who you need to watch out for.

Graham Graves, 2002

Author's Note

A Vampire in Our Midst

In the summer of 1999, Jenna Prescott attempted to murder her stepfather, Joe Murphy. Her boyfriend, Peter Kilmer, was set to take part in the murder with her but backed out at the last moment. He was the one that ended up calling the cops on Jenna when she was on her way home from his house to her own, where she intended on stabbing her stepfather—a task at which she was successful, just not successful enough. Jenna's original plan had been to involve several of her friends in the murder. Ultimately she only succeeded in getting her fourteen-year-old cousin to accompany her. Noelle Prescott would go on to testify for the prosecution in Jenna Prescott's trial, sealing Jenna's fate and putting her behind bars for the next twenty years.

The case grabbed national headlines and certainly made waves here in my home state of Oklahoma, seeing as how it occurred in one of the most affluent and historic suburbs in Oklahoma City. The house where it happened still stands. Jenna's family lives there to this day.

There was one particular detail about Jenna's case that caught my attention. For employment, I host a late-night paranormal radio show featuring callers that detail encounters with all manner of otherworldly things. So, it was the fact that Jenna claimed to be a three-hundred-year-old vampire that really reached out and grabbed me.

It turned out that Jenna was running a game with her friends in which they participated in vampire role-playing.

In the game, Jenna played a vampire named Josephine and even insisted on her friends calling her by her vampire name. Other players of the game included her cousin, Noelle Prescott, her boyfriend, Peter Kilmer, a friend, Heather Frakes, a friend, Travis

James, and a friend, Nolan Jennings. The group met weekly to play Vampires: the Hunted. Over time, the game came to mean more to them all than just a role-playing meetup.

The group would sometimes engage in blood-play, cutting each other and drinking one another's blood. Psychologist's have said that it was a power play on Jenna Prescott's part. She wanted the group to feel as if they were inextricably bound together. That idea leads to the question: had she planned the murder from the very beginning?

I'm of a mind to think that she hadn't. I think the murder was secondary to the formation of the group, but hardly a result of its existence. Plenty of people play roleplaying games—even taking them extremely seriously—without committing murder or attempting to.

Still, the thought that someone as young as Noelle Prescott could become wrapped up in something like this is enough to give any parent pause.

It was this crime that led me down the path of wanting to write this book. Vampires have long fascinated me and on my radio program, they rarely come up, though they sometimes do. This feels like an area of the unexplained that I've left unexplored for a bit too long, and nothing would delight me more than to discover a *real* vampire. Not just someone who claims to be one.

When I first started writing this book, I put out a

message on a message board, asking if anyone knew of any real vampires or had an encounter with one. Immediately, I was getting emails. Most of them were dismissible, but some weren't. Some of them felt like they were authentic encounters. Even one where someone claimed to have met the elusive Count St. Germain in New Orleans at Halloween a few years ago.

But there was one email that stood out to me during those first few days. The writer went by the surname of the most famous Count himself.

Dracula.

To: g.graves@yahoo.com

From: mrdracula@yahoo.com

Subject: Searching for my kind

Dear Mr. Graves,

I've been a listener of your show for some time now, though not anywhere near as long as I've survived on this planet. You see, I'm a *real* vampire. The kind that you seek. I am approximately five-hundred years old. I've used the pseudonym Dracula for our correspondence because I do not wish for you to discover who I truly am because what I'm going to tell you is alarming. I want to give you an account of my life, and that includes instances of what you might consider murder.

If this is something that you'd be interested
in hearing, I'll look forward to your reply.
Mr. D

The email caught me off guard. Most of the emails
from people claiming to be vampires came off as
unhinged or as the work of a prankster. But there was
something about this email that made me want to know
more. So, I wrote Mr. D back.

And so began the correspondence that would form
somewhat of a quest for me. Mr D's emails followed
me throughout the writing of this tome. I hope that
you'll enjoy his tale as much as I did, and perhaps by
the end of the book, you will make up your own mind
about whether he was, as he claimed, a *real* vampire.

As for me, the jury is still out. I like to keep an open
mind.

That being said, I won't be sad if I never hear from
him again.

CHAPTER SIX

I STAY up into the night making notes on my dad's book. And by the time I finish the first chapter, I'm intrigued by the Mr. D that my dad corresponded with. The rest of chapter one went on to explain more about Jenna's case and even included a quote from Peter Kilmer. Apparently, my dad interviewed him shortly after Jenna's trial.

I make notes, creating the bare bones of an outline for Cash's research. I focus on Jenna's case, sure that he's going to want to cover it in at least one of the episodes he's going to do. But my mind keeps drifting back to Mr. D, and I'm eager to get another chance to sit down with my father's book and see what happened with all of that. I have to remind myself that the reason I'm doing this research has to do with Cash and not my own personal interest. Although, what would it hurt if I *was* interested in it?

There's no denying that I've had fun with Cash. In both of our adventures. Maybe this is another one, although I hope not. Something about a vampire adventure seems a little more ominous than one involving a haunted house or a Sasquatch.

I shake the idea from my mind and conclude that I'm just freaking myself out. I find my way to bed and in the morning, I go over my notes, ready to get started again. But it's as I'm having coffee, getting my motor running again that I get a notification on my phone from Cash.

Thought you might want to know about this

I stare at the text for a second, processing it. I'm not all the way awake. But before I can analyze it further, a link to a news article pops up in our thread. I look at the little picture preview. It's a set of vampire fangs with blood dripping from them, almost looking like what you might see in a Halloween store advertisement. But this isn't an ad. I read the title of the article.

Metro woman slain in vampire-like killing
My eyebrows shoot up.

When did this happen?

I text back before I open the article. I don't wait for Cash's response. I go in and read it.

Oklahoma City, Oklahoma — 13 October. Authorities are working to identify the body of a woman found near Lake Draper overnight. Details about the body include puncture wounds on the victim's neck and a massive amount of blood loss. A local teenager stumbled across the body while out at the lake with friends last night. They called the police and detectives have begun an investigation into the death. At this time, it appears to be a homicide, though there are no leads yet. The vampire-like slaying comes only two weeks before Halloween, making people speculate about the nature of the killing and whether there might be another. Police say at this time there is no reason for public concern.

I go back to the message thread.

Last night

Cash's message comes through just as I start typing a response to the article.

Weird for this to happen right after Jenna gets out of prison

I wait for his response. He types something, then

deletes it. The little text bubble disappears and reappears twice, making me think he's choosing his words carefully. He probably doesn't want to say anything bad about Noelle and he's narrowly avoiding it.

Meet for breakfast?

I text him back and tell him *sure*. We make plans to meet at the little twenty-four-hour diner right down the street from my house called The Full Moon. The neon sign outside has a wolf howling up at the object of its affection. It's a bit of a drive for him, but he seems eager to talk about this. And besides, he likes their pancakes.

I put away my laptop and get ready in a hurry, just as eager to talk about this with him as he is with me. I throw on a sweater and some jeans and slip into a pair of boots that I left by the door. And then I head out for the diner.

I snag a table once there and wait for Cash. In just a few minutes, he pulls up outside in his massive truck. I thought, the first time I met him, that it was a substitute for masculinity. But after I saw how tall Cash is, I realized it was probably one of the few vehicles that accommodated his size properly.

He gets out and the bell rings as he opens the glass door of the diner. I wave at him and he spots me.

"Good morning, Miss Graves," Cash says as he stoops and slides into the booth across from me.

"Mr. Kelly," I say with a smirk.

"So, what did you think about that news article?" He cuts right to the chase.

"What can I get for the two of you?" Our waitress sneaks up on us and I startle, almost jumping in my seat. Must be all the vampire stuff I've read in the last twenty-four hours. It's enough to put ideas in your head, even in broad daylight in the middle of a diner.

"Coffee and water, please," I say. Cash tells her he wants the same. Then I order a breakfast burrito with hash browns, and he gets pancakes and every side imaginable. She disappears back into the kitchen, leaving us to pick up the rest of the vampire conversation.

"Well?" Cash asks.

"Well, what?" I ask.

"The story," he says, rolling his eyes, exasperated that my brain isn't running as quickly as his this morning. Apparently only one of us stayed up into the wee hours of the night with my dad's book as their only company. Probably a mistake, but here we are.

"Oh, yeah," I say. "It's just crazy to me that it would happen *now* of all times," I tell him. I lean forward in my seat as I say the last part of the sentence and I glance over my shoulder afterwards, making sure no one's staring at us. But the coast is clear.

"That was my thought exactly," Cash says. "It's got to be connected."

"Connected how?" I ask. "Jenna acted alone.

There was only one attempted murder, and it was her trying to kill her stepfather. That seems like a pretty clear-cut case to me. No loose ends," I say.

"It might be someone that was inspired by her," Cash says. "Maybe the murder was their way to celebrate her getting out of prison."

I roll this over in my mind.

"That's crazy," I mutter. But there's a small part of me that doesn't want to be so quick to dismiss the idea.

"Is it, though?" Cash asks.

He's got a point. We're talking about someone that used to pretend she was a three-hundred-year-old vampire. Anything is possible.

"I started on the research for you last night. Found my dad's book," I say. "There's a lot about Jenna in it. A lot I didn't know." The last almost comes out bitterly. There's a small sliver of my mind that's a little annoyed at everything Noelle didn't tell me. But rationally I know it's her story to do with as she wishes. She doesn't owe it to anyone. Not even me.

"How's it coming?" Cash asks. "Are you regretting taking the job yet?" He smirks, but I can tell he's only halfway kidding.

"Why would I regret it?" I ask with a laugh.

"It can get weird sometimes," he says. "But anyway, you were reading your dad's book, huh?"

"Yeah," I say. "*Love in the Time of Vampires*."

"That's not the title of that book," he says with a furrowed brow.

"But wouldn't it be more fun if it was?" I tease.

"I think *The Beautiful and the Dead* was a fine title," he says, mentioning the actual title of the book. "Plays off of some F. Scott Fitzgerald vibes."

"You would like that, wouldn't you?" I smirk.

"Anyway," Cash says. "How's it coming? And seriously, are you regretting it yet?"

"No regrets," I tell him. "Yet," I add. "And it's coming along nicely. There's a lot I didn't know. Not just about Jenna, but about vampires in general."

"A lot of people dismiss things like vampires and werewolves as folklore or as scary stories to tell kids at night, but there's a lot more to it than that. It's really quite fascinating," he says.

He's not wrong. I found myself really enjoying the research I was able to do last night. Enjoying it a lot more than I thought I would, actually. And more than I'm willing to admit to Cash just yet.

"It is," I say. "But back to the murder..."

"Yeah," he says. "It's just too weird for there to be no connection to Jenna."

"Do you think the cops will seek her out?" My eyes widen at the thought. I was just having dinner with her the other night, and now I'm suggesting that the police should be questioning her about a murder that just happened.

"If they've got even a degree of common sense," Cash says. "I can't imagine being a detective and not making the connection between her case and this one. I mean, how often is it that you get a vampire killing anywhere, let alone Oklahoma City?"

"Good point," I say. "They'd be crazy not to look into it."

I suddenly have the itch to talk to Noelle. I wonder if she's been in contact with Jenna since the party. Our texting hasn't been as usual. Something's up and my gut tells me it's Jenna. I'm worried they've been hanging out.

"You should ask Noelle," Cash says, as if reading my mind. "See what she'll tell you."

"I'm not sure she'd tell me much," I admit. "You should have seen her the other night. *Bam!* Right back under Jenna's spell," I say with a snap of my fingers. "It was eerie to watch."

"I can only imagine," Cash says.

Just then his phone vibrates on the table. He reaches down for it and reads something on the screen.

"Wow," he mutters. "I don't think we're going to have to wait for you to talk to Noelle to find out if Jenna's going to hear from the police," he says. He looks up at me.

"What?" I ask.

"My friend who works at the newspaper just updated me on things. He just got the victim's name. They identified her," he says.

"Who was it?" I'm on pins and needles.

"Heather Frakes," he says. "As in the same Heather

Frakes that used to play Vampires: the Hunted alongside no one other than Jenna Prescott."

My eyes widen and I feel like I'm going to be sick.

THE STORY HASN'T BROKEN OFFICIALLY YET, so there's no way that Noelle would know about it. Unless, of course, Jenna *does* know something about it and she's told Noelle. In which case, I don't know that I want to know.

The whole thing has my stomach in a knot once I get back to the house. I pace up and down the hallway, debating on whether I should reach out to Noelle with the news or not. Finally, I come to a decision and type out a simple text to test the waters.

> Hey, how are you?

It's innocent enough and gives her the opportunity to tell me anything she might know without me having to ask for it. I'm not super hopeful, though. Not after watching her with Jenna the other night.

I sit there with the thread open for a couple of minutes, waiting to hear back from Noelle. Finally, just as I'm about to close out of the message, I see the little bubble with blinking dots that lets me know she's typing out a response.

It seems like it takes forever, but finally, it comes through.

I'm good! How are you?

Her reply is clipped, unlike her. Normally, she would be giving me a run-down of everything that had happened since I last saw her. Something's up. I have a sick feeling that I already know what it is.

I write her back without telling her what I'm up to on Cash's behalf. I don't really feel like explaining myself and I also feel like treading into the vampire territory might make her not want to talk to me even more.

Good.

I stare at the message. A single word. It's not how Noelle and I usually communicate. She's got to feel it, too.

Hey I was meaning to ask you if you'd like to come to the housewarming party I'm throwing.

I stare at the text. It's strange, her asking me if I want to come. It feels like just one more divide between the two of us. Normally, I'd be the one helping her plan it. I wasn't even aware she wanted to have a party at her new place.

I answer her and get the details and ask if I can bring Cash. My reasoning is that if Jenna's there, I don't want to be a third wheel all night. I don't tell

Noelle that, though. It would also be nice to have someone there who could tell me if I'm overreacting.

It also strikes me that Noelle didn't phrase it as a question. It was a statement.

Normally, she'd punctuate something like that with a question mark. It's like she's hesitant. Or thinks that I'll say *no*. Which only makes me more suspicious about what she's been up to.

And specifically, who she's been with.

We'll be there.

I send the simple response. Noelle puts a heart reaction on it but says nothing else. Another strike making me think she's keeping something from me.

The whole situation is about to make me crazy. With that in mind, I put my phone away and decide to get back to researching vampires for Cash. Maybe that will put my mind at ease.

Hah! Not likely.

But at least it might serve as a distraction.

CHAPTER SEVEN

I BURY myself in research for the majority of the morning and early afternoon. I hate to admit that I find it soothing. I can certainly understand the satisfaction my dad got from this. It occurs to me that it's one of the first instances I've ever found myself thinking that I might understand something about my father. The thought brings a sad smile to my face. Just eight years too late, Blair.

The thought casts a bitterness over the warm realization of why my dad enjoyed research. I try to shake it off, forcing thoughts of him and our relationship out of my mind. Today, I'm not diving back into his book. Instead, I'm doing some digging on the internet.

I do some searches for various things: vampires, vampires in America, undead encounters, vampire encounters, vampire folklore, vampire history, famous vampires, real vampires.

And it's on the last one that I get a hit that truly piques my interest.

Vampire's Ball — a message board for real vampires

I stare at the result for a moment and almost hesitate on clicking it. Something deep in my gut tells me that it's probably not the safest online space I could venture into. But I'm browsing, anonymous. What can it hurt?

I click on the link.

It takes me to a website that looks like it might have been created back in the days of Geocities and Angel-Fire. Pixelated torches line either side of the page and dance as I scroll through the various boards. And there are a number of them. A banner proudly declares that there are fifty-four users online now. Another banner indicates how many hits the website has gotten over the years, and judging by the appearance of the web design, it's been around for a minute or two. The number reads somewhere in the millions.

I wonder how many of those hits are distinct individuals and how many are returning users, refreshing the boards for new information. I'm not sure old counters like that make much of a distinction.

The background of the site is a graphic of a dungeon. I start looking at the names of the various boards.

Vampires 101, Donors, Fangs, Lifestyle, Fashion, Pop Culture, News.

I decide to click on the Vampires 101 board and

see what messages have been posted. I'm also curious to see how recently those messages have been posted and with what kind of frequency. I wonder if the website is still in high use.

A list of posts pops up and I begin to read them.

New to the scene

Help! What kind of vampire am I?

Are psychic vampires real? And how do I get rid of one?

Drinking blood and safety

I balk at the last one. I know I read it in my dad's book that sometimes Jenna would make people exchange blood but seeing it here on the website shocks me a little. The idea that people might be sharing their blood with strangers makes my stomach queasy. Surely to God they're safe about it. I imagine the majority are.

But I know people. And people aren't known for their great common sense.

Especially when it comes to safety.

I shudder at the thought.

I go back to the previous page and my cursor hovers over the Donors page. I wonder what fresh hell awaits me there. I can't help myself, and I click it.

I'm not disappointed.

Looking for single, clean female in
    Detroit area

Seeking black swan in Los Angeles

Black swans wanted in NYC area

Dayton, OH — will compensate for
    blood

Jesus Christ.

I do a quick search in another browser window for the term *black swan* as it relates to vampire subculture. Apparently, it's a human that offers themselves as a blood donor for an active vampire.

It makes me wonder what other terminology there is.

I switch back to the vampire message board.

I scan the list, looking for Oklahoma. I'm relieved when I don't see it. But there is a plethora of pages after this one, so there's no telling how many times someone from the Sooner State has posted looking for a blood donor.

Yikes.

The posts are recent, all of them on the front page within the last week. That leads me to believe the site is still pretty active. I would find that more surprising if it weren't for the fact that a woman died in Oklahoma City less than twenty-four hours ago under suspicious, vampire-like circumstances. That murder drives it home that there are still people who participate in the lifestyle and not just on the fun level. Some of them take it too far.

It reminds me of the quote about staring too long into the abyss.

That thought sends a shiver down my spine.

I go back to the main page and a thought occurs to me. I bet there's chatter on the News board about Jenna Prescott getting out of prison. I wonder how people inside the vampire lifestyle look at her. If they see her as a martyr or a crazy person that took a good time beyond the pale.

And when the page loads, my suspicion is confirmed.

The page is chock full of posts about Jenna being released from prison.

They range from celebratory to scornful.

I click on one of them.

Y'all should be ashamed of yourselves making her out to be some kind of hero. Maybe this is an unpopular opinion, but Jenna Prescott gave the whole lifestyle a bad rap. Tell me I'm wrong.

There are a few others like that on the main page.

And then there are those that seem to see her release from prison as some kind of vampire victory.

The queen is free! Thank the gods they let Miss Prescott out of prison. She did nothing wrong, was only acting on her natural instincts to kill. Vampires should have a different set of laws that apply to them! Call your congressman!

There are posts even more unhinged than that one declaring Jenna's release a win for vampires everywhere. They wish her well and some of them even talk about making plans to come to Oklahoma City to try to meet her. The thought is disturbing. It's like she's some kind of celebrity to them.

I keep scrolling and then I see something that catches my eye.

A long time coming

That's the post title. I click on it. And then I begin to read.

I did something last night that I can't tell anyone about except you guys. I finally acted on my instincts. I had my first kill. I drank her blood and it was so sweet, tangy. I drained her.

She didn't even put up much of a fight. I was sort of surprised. This has been a long time coming. I'm glad she got to enjoy one last sunset at the lake first.

The lake. The murder.

My heart pounds in my chest.

Did I just stumble across a genuine murder confession?

I READ the post four times, making sure that I'm interpreting it the right way. The thought occurs to me that this could be a typical post on these message boards. There might be role-players here. Or trolls. I start combing through the other pages, looking for similar posts.

But I don't find any. This one seems to be a rarity.

Which only lends to its credibility, doesn't it?

I remind myself that this could be a prank. A teenager could have written that after reading one too many of Anne Rice's books. Or having played too many video games. There's every chance that the post is nothing to be concerned about and I need to keep my feet on the ground.

Still, it's alarming.

I pick up the phone and call Cash. I don't bother with a text message. I want to talk to him *now*.

"Hello?" He picks up on the first ring.

"I have something to show you," I say.

"What is it?" Cash asks.

"Just come over. Now," I tell him. "I think I just read a murder confession."

CHAPTER EIGHT

CASH GETS HERE in record time, apparently as startled as I was by my find. He jogs up the steps and I have the door open for him by the time he's on the porch.

"Come in," I say.

"Where's this murder confession?" Cash asks.

He doesn't even bother shrugging out of his leather jacket while I lead him to the living room where I've got my little research station set up. I indicate that he should sit down in front of the computer. I lean over him and point at the post.

"I found this message board. It's for 'real' vampires, whatever that means. Anyway, I went to this part, the News section," I click the link. "And I found this." I navigate him to the post and I click on it. I sit down on the other side of the couch and let him read the post.

I watch his expression as he does so. It's pure

concentration, focus. A furrowing of the skin between his eyebrows, then suddenly, his eyes go wide. He looks at me.

"Whoa," he says.

"So, I'm not crazy?" I ask. "It sounds like the murder that happened at the lake!"

"That was my first thought," Cash says.

Cash pokes around on the message board some more.

"Was there any indication of who posted it?" Cash asks.

"Right there, under the message there's a user-name," I say.

"Dracula87," Cash reads the name out loud.

"I guess it's a vampire that was born in 1987? The same year as me," I say.

"Your guess is as good as mine," Cash says.

"Do you think a man or a woman wrote it?" I ask.

"There's not really any way to tell from the post," Cash says. He rereads it, his lips forming the words silently as he goes. "It could be a man or a woman. Or hell, it could be some teenager, getting kicks out of this sort of thing."

"Isn't it weird, though, that it popped up before the story broke?" I ask.

Cash seems to contemplate that.

He nods.

"That *is* weird," he says.

"Right?" There's something about the post that

strikes me as genuine. I don't really have any way of putting my finger on what it is. I keep going over it in my mind and come up empty handed. There's just something about it. And maybe that's just me making things up in my head, but I have a bad feeling about it.

"And weird that they mention the lake," Cash adds. "That seems like an oddly specific detail to throw in there for someone that was just pulling a prank. It's almost like whoever posted it is hoping to breadcrumb anyone from the area that might stumble on the post,"

A dark thought occurs to me.

Someone who would leave a clue like that might have the intention to do this again. And if that's the case, how many more times would they do it again? More than two? If that's the case, then we're going to have a serial killer on our hands. That would be a grim day for the city. And I can't imagine that it wouldn't make national news with the nature of the killing.

"You don't think..." I trail off, not sure if I should even be voicing a worry like this. Like somehow that might make it come to fruition.

But Cash beats me to it.

"You're thinking it might be a serial killer, aren't you?" he asks.

I nod my head solemnly. That's *exactly* what I'm thinking.

"I'm afraid of that," I tell him, not speaking very loudly. I feel like if I do, the universe will hear it and make it a reality. Like somehow, I'd be manifesting a serial killer right here in Oklahoma City.

"I'm afraid of that, too," Cash says, his tone somber. I feel less crazy worrying about it now that he's voiced the opinion that it could be a possibility. It's both reassuring and not. I wish he'd said something like *that's insane*. Or *there's no way*. But he didn't.

And that concerns me.

"It's got to be someone affiliated with Jenna," I say. Heather Frakes is too close a connection for this *not* to have something to do with Jenna's release from prison. Noelle might be in danger. My heart beats faster. I look at Cash, sure that concern is etched on my features.

The expression on *his* face does nothing to reassure me. He furrows his brow, looks up at me and speaks.

"It certainly seems that way," Cash says.

I swallow, thinking he's right. And I'm concerned about that idea.

I rack my brain, trying to think of the people that were affiliated with Jenna and the vampire game. I think of her ex-boyfriend, Peter. One of the people that testified to put her away. I can't imagine that he'd have anything to do with it. It seems like he did everything he could to escape her reach. But then again, I don't know the guy. I don't know what his possible motivations for this could be.

Whoever it is, I'm worried about Noelle.

I think about her spending time with Jenna. That can't be good. That can't be healthy.

I wonder if she's with Jenna right now.

"What are you thinking about?" Cash asks me, breaking the spell I'm under.

"I'm thinking about Noelle," I tell him. I bite the inside of my lip.

"It's understandable that you'd be worried, Blair," he says. There's understanding on his face. Along with empathy.

I try to calm myself down. Tell myself that there's nothing to worry about. Maybe the fact that Heather was killed is just a coincidence. But I know it's not. It can't be. How many people in this state have a criminal past and a connection to the vampire scene?

Not many, I'm guessing.

It's enough to keep me up tonight.

"You don't think Jenna herself was involved, do you?" Cash asks. "Do you think she's capable of something like that? Would she take that chance? Maybe as revenge for all the time she spent in prison?"

"I mean, she did stab her stepfather. A *lot*," I say.

Cash chuckles.

"You have a point," he says.

There's no mirth in his laughter. It's grim. The whole situation seems grim. But then I try to turn it around.

"Hey, maybe we shouldn't go down this road just yet," I say. "We don't really even know anything yet other than what your friend told you."

Cash seems to think this over for a moment.

"You're probably right," he says. "Hell, there may not be another murder like this. We won't know until it happens," he adds. "There's no point in obsessing about it now. That being said, I think we need to call the cops about that post," he finishes. "Maybe there's some other explanation for what happened to Heather. Maybe she's still in the scene and this is someone unrelated to Jenna," Cash goes on. "But we definitely need to report this."

"I think you're right," I say. And I grab my phone.

THERE'S a knock at the door shortly after I call. We probably only wait about twenty minutes.

I swing it wide and a detective wearing a gray suit is standing on my porch.

"Good evening," he says as I open the door. He doesn't bother offering me a smile. I wonder if detectives ever really get to smile at people when they're on the clock.

My guess is *probably not*.

"Come in," I say.

Cash stands in the entry hall next to the fountain. He crosses his arms and leans against the wall.

"You must be Miss Graves, and this must be Mr. Kelly," the detective says. "I'm Detective Garcia. I understand that the two of you found what you believe to be a confession on a..." he pulls a notebook out of his pocket and looks at it. "Message board?"

The way he says it puts a knot in my stomach. Like he's not taking this seriously at all. Doubt slips into my mind. Am I overreacting? It could be an innocent post. Well, as innocent as pretending to confess to murder can be. It might be some teenager, and the lake was just a detail they threw in. The chances that they're actually from Oklahoma City are slim.

"Yes," I say.

"Can I see the post?" the detective asks.

I show him to the living room and pull it up on my computer. I let him sit down and he begins reading it, studying it hard. Finally, he speaks.

"It's certainly something," the detective says. He leans back from the screen, and I don't like the tone of his voice. It's clear he isn't taking it seriously.

"Couldn't that be a confession to a real murder?" I ask.

"It could," he says. "But on a message board like this, where people come to role-play as vampires, it's less compelling. If he'd posted it on Facebook, I might sing a different tune."

I look at Cash and widen my eyes then nod toward the detective.

Cash clears his throat.

"But don't you think the detail about the lake is significant?" Cash asks.

"It could be, but there's nothing else that makes me think this has anything to do with anything going on in the city," he says. "By the way, how did the two of you know about the vampire murder at the lake?"

Cash and I exchange a glance, both of us trying to figure out if we should tell the truth. I let Cash take the lead.

"A friend of mine at a newspaper told me," Cash says. He looks down at his boots and then back up at the detective, as if he's daring him to give him shit for that. The detective seems to decide not to.

"Good to know they still pass on the news the minute they get it," the detective says sarcastically.

He stands up from his seat on the couch.

"I would tell the two of you that this is likely nothing to worry about. I'll take down the web address for the post if we end up needing it, but I think you might be worrying pointlessly."

I nod, feeling like we're being totally dismissed. At least he's taking down notes of how to get back to the site. That's at least something.

After he finishes jotting in his notepad, he closes it and sticks it into the pocket of his jacket.

"I'll show you out," Cash says. There's a bitterness to his tone that lets me know he doesn't think much of this guy's detective work, either.

Detective Garcia follows Cash down the hallway. Cash looms over him at the door, like an imposing statue guarding the entrance to my house. Garcia thanks us for our time, though I'm relatively certain he's annoyed that we took up any of his. Cash closes the door and turns to face me.

"Well," he says. "That's that I guess." He sounds frustrated.

"It doesn't have to be," I say with a smirk.

"Are you thinking what I'm thinking?" Cash asks.

"Maybe your vampire video series could include this story," I say. "So, we wouldn't just be nosing around. We'd be helping to educate the public."

Cash nods, false solemnity in his gesture.

"Yeah, nothing to do with our own personal interests," he adds with a smile.

"Let's see what we can figure out," I tell him.

And then we head back to the living room, and he sheds his jacket, taking a seat next to me in front of my laptop.

CHAPTER NINE

THE STORY BREAKS LATE that night. It's all over the news, probably for a few reasons. It's unusual, for one. For another, Halloween is on the horizon. It's the kind of thing the news probably only sees in wet dreams. It makes my stomach turn a little bit when I see the first article about it pop up in my social media feeds. There's also the fact that the news has connected Heather Frakes to Jenna Prescott.

I give it a little while then I shoot Noelle a text.

You up?

It's not that late, but I don't want to call her if she's busy. And my gut tells me that if she's with Jenna, she isn't going to answer me. Better that way, really. The questions I have in mind to ask her aren't any that I want her to have an audience for. Particularly not an audience comprised of Jenna Prescott and whoever else might be with them.

I sit my phone down on the end table next to me. My laptop is still sitting open and Cash has gone home. I didn't really want to have this conversation with him present, either. I just wanted a moment between me and Noelle. I know there's a good chance that she's not going to tell me exactly what's going on or what she's been up to. I just want the chance to talk to her, one on one.

I turn on the television and keep glancing at my phone, hoping that one of these times that I look at it, the screen will be illuminated with a notification letting me know that Noelle has replied.

I am. What's up?

Her answer is curt. Much shorter than I hoped it would be but it's exactly what I was bracing myself for. I feel my stomach flutter as I start typing out my response, reminding myself that I need to tread lightly.

I hate feeling like there's this divide between the two of us. Noelle and I have always been close. The kind of close where we tell each other anything and everything. Even if it's too much information some-times. It feels weird now. I don't like it at all.

I type out several responses, trying to gage the situation. I try on each of them, my finger hovering over the send button. But ultimately, I delete them all. Finally, I settle on something simple. Innocuous.

Or at least innocuous enough.

> I was just thinking about you. How are you doing?

I hope it doesn't show my hand, but if Noelle is watching the news at all, I'm not sure how it won't.

I bite my lip, staring at the screen, waiting for the little dots to pop up, pulsing and letting me know that Noelle is typing something. It doesn't happen immediately. But I keep the thread open. Finally, I see the little indicator letting me know I'm not alone in the chat.

I feel my stomach drop, waiting for her answer. I don't know what I'm expecting—for her to tell me to go fuck myself?—but the feeling that I'm on her bad side is strong. I can only imagine what she and Jenna have been saying to each other. And I can only imagine just how far Jenna has already pulled her back under her wing.

Surely Noelle wouldn't let that happen.

She's smart. She's strong.

But I also know that monsters can be wily. Monsters can be crafty in ways that the rest of us would never imagine.

And I worry about that.

The news story hangs between us, suspended in the ether. I try to think of how to bring it up without immediately sounding like I'm playing her protective older sister.

> I'm good! I was actually about to text you.

This piques my interest. Text me? About what?

I watch as the little bubble pops up letting me know she's typing.

> I wanted to see if you'd bring a couple of bottles of wine to the housewarming party :)

The phrasing bothers me. It's so casual. And then I realize I have no one to blame for that but myself. I toss the phone down and groan.

I'd completely disregarded any role she might have wanted me to play in her housewarming party. I should have been texting her about it. She probably thinks I don't care. I pick my phone back up.

I tap out a response, then delete it, then tap out another one.

I do this a few times, just like earlier, and finally, I settle on one.

> Yes, of course. Do you need any more help?

It's less personal than it should be. It feels stilted. The whole interaction does. I feel my heart begin to sink when she responds.

No, I've got some help! But thank you! I'll see you guys there!

It feels like a punch to the gut. I drop my phone again, unsure of what else to say. I didn't even manage to feel out the situation about Jenna. However, I'm pretty sure that's the *help* she referenced. A realization that makes my skin crawl.

Maybe that makes me a bad friend.

It wouldn't be the first time.

CHAPTER TEN

FRIDAY ROLLS AROUND and Cash shows up right on time to pick me up. I sigh and check my lipstick one last time in the hallway mirror. I fluff my hair and realize that I'm fussing over my appearance. Something that I don't normally do. And something that makes me uneasy. Has my subconscious mind been straying down that primrose path about what's going on between Cash and me?

I try to remember what I dreamt about last night. Nothing immediately comes to mind. But there's the faintest memory of skin on skin. Lips on mine. My eyes meet themselves in the mirror and I see a flush spread from my collarbone up to my hairline.

Shit. Well, I guess we know what the dream was about.

The realization gives me a haunted look that I do my best to wipe off my face. I clear my throat. I'm a grown woman. I'm allowed to have sex dreams. So what if it was about my new boss?

I mean, that is what he is now, isn't it?

Jesus Christ.

My new boss. My dad's former employee. YouTube sensation. Six-and-a-half foot tall Cash Kelly. A giant, extremely handsome oak tree of a man that just needs someone to climb him.

Blair!

I clear my throat again, shocked at my internal dialogue. I grab my purse and throw the door open before I can go any further down that path. But as soon as I crawl up inside the darkened cab of his truck, I'm hit by the faint scent of his aftershave and the thoughts return. I fight the urge to verbally banish them.

"You look good," Cash says in the darkness. There's a husky quality to his voice that makes the blush from earlier return.

I look over at him in the darkness. Green light from the dash illuminates his features. I make out the harsh line of his jaw and the faintest hint of a five o'clock shadow. One hand rests on the wheel, the other is casually atop the console. I'm suddenly conscious of my own body and I clasp my hands in my lap.

"Thank you," I say, staring straight forward. "You look good, too."

The response comes out more formally than I mean for it to. But he does look good. Even though I only caught a glimpse of him in the dash light it's enough to know that his black shirt is clinging to the muscles of his arms. Arms that were tangled with my own in my dream last night.

My breath hitches in my chest.

"You okay?" Cash asks as he pulls out of the driveway.

"Fine," I say, casting a smile over at him. I find my eyes trailing down the length of his arm, noticing the size of his hands in a way I haven't before. I imagine them in a darkened room, sliding beneath the hem of my shirt.

Fuck.

My eyes widen and I look straight forward again.

"You sure you're okay?" Cash asks with a nervous laugh.

"I'm fine," I banish all sexual thoughts about him.

It's crossed my mind before, but never this intensely. I look over at him and smile, telling myself that I've got control of the situation now. But he smiles at me, and I see the shadow in his dimple in the darkness. It pierces through me in the black cab of the truck.

We drive in companionable silence all the way to Noelle's, me interjecting directions here and there. Finally, we pull up outside her house and get out of the truck.

The October air is chilly, even though I'm wearing a plaid flannel over my white t-shirt. There are cars parked up and down the street. I can hear the sounds of people laughing and music playing on the patio out back of Noelle's house. Cash walks around to the passenger side of the truck where I stand.

"Let's go," he says after a beat.

I realize then that I'm standing in the street staring up at the house. There's a part of me that doesn't want to go in. I don't want to see Jenna again. Even though I barely know her she made me feel uneasy and there's no denying that. Even more than that, I don't want to see Noelle under her spell.

It's insane to me that Noelle is having her here with Heather Frakes dead at the Medical Examiner's Office.

But the only way I'm going to know how she's doing is by setting foot in that house.

I sigh and look at Cash.

"Let's go," I say.

He does something then that surprises me. He stands a pace or two in front of me and he reaches a hand back for me. Out of instinct, I reach for his hand and grab it. His palm is warm, dry, and swallows mine whole. My heart jumps to my throat. I wonder if he can feel my pulse through my fingertips and I pray he can't.

We walk together and he glances over at me, smiling slightly. I look away instantly. The expression makes me suddenly aware of my entire body. I feel like it's on fire. I feel my heart skipping like a stone over water. It's something I hadn't expected, especially not tonight.

We walk together, hand in hand, up to the porch. I feel the crunch of dead grass under my Doc Martens. I hear it beneath Cash's boots, too. Noelle has a red bulb in the porch fixture, and it casts a romantic glow over Cash's features when we make it to the door. He stops, turning to me.

I reach for the doorbell, punching it before I look at Cash.

"Blair," he says, my hand in his.

I look over at him. The red light from the fixture illuminates him in soft shades. His face is pink, his features almost blurred smoothly. There's something in his eyes that at once seems familiar and strange. An expression I'm not sure I've seen there before. A small smile curves one side of his mouth. He lets out a chuckle and rubs his stubble with his free hand.

"I'm glad you decided to work with me," he says. He looks down at his boots as he speaks. "You know... you, uh, mean..."

"There you are!" Noelle appears at the doorway instantly, breaking the spell of the moment. Cash drops my hand and it falls heavy at my side. I want it to still be in his. I feel naked, exposed. I force a smile at Noelle. She looks from me to Cash and back again. "Oh, am I interrupting something?" she asks, sounding somewhat nervous.

"No," I say.

"No, no," Cash affirms at the same time.

But I look over at him. And it's only for a moment. A split second. But I feel the emotion that passes between us, and I think I know what he was about to say before Noelle opened the door.

"Okay, well," Noelle smiles at both of us but I can tell she's self-conscious, thinking that she interrupted us.

"You look adorable," I tell her and sweep her into a hug, hoping that the gesture will negate any of the weirdness between the two of us. And she hugs me back, but there's something false about it. Even with her body pressed against mine, it feels like there's a wall between us.

I pull back, my hands on her shoulders, and I search her face. But she steps away and shakes Cash's hand, greeting him.

I hang back and she leads us into the house. There are people everywhere.

"Hooper brought a bunch of his friends from work," Noelle says over her shoulder to me.

Suddenly, I feel like an even worse friend. I wonder if Hooper is staying with her. I should know this, but I don't. I've been too wrapped up in what I've been doing with Cash. And now isn't the time to ask.

But I spot Hooper as we make our way through the kitchen and Noelle gets a beer for each of us. I wave at Hooper and he waves back, then continues his conversation with a group of guys he's standing with.

My eyes scan the room and I take a sip of my beer.

"I'm so glad you guys could make it," Noelle says with a smile to me.

She squeezes my hand then. The first genuinely warm gesture I've felt from her since the night I went with her to that dinner party.

"Me, too," I say. "Everything looks—"

"There you are."

I recognize the voice instantly. The same candy-coated sickly sweetness from the other night. Jenna.

I turn to see her and Noelle drops my hand. It happens instantly. I feel Jenna's energy envelope Noelle right there in front of me, like she's a baby bird being swept under her mother's wing. Except in this example, the mother bird in question is actually a harpy.

Jenna smiles at me. On the outside, it's all warmth and vibrance. But there's a coldness to it that I think anyone with a set of eyes and a good gut instinct could pick up on. It worries me that Noelle seems to be ignoring it.

Noelle steps to her side, almost like she's choosing sides on a battle. I hate that it feels this way. Like some weird cold war between the two of us. My eyes don't leave Jenna's, though.

Her smile falters. It's momentary, but just enough. I see through the facade. I see pain and anger there. And I wonder how much of that anger she wants to direct at Noelle.

The thought stirs butterflies in my gut. Not the good kind. These feel more like bats stirring in their belfry, about to announce that their beloved Dracula has come home to roost.

And just like that, Jenna spins and takes Noelle off to some other part of the party, leaving me and Cash in her wake. I watch as they go and think this is going to be a long night.

CASH WALKS over beside me after they leave us. He towers over me and sips his beer.

"So that's her, huh?" he asks.

"That's her," I confirm.

"Somehow, she's smaller than I imagined," Cash remarks.

"What did you expect? A giant like you?" I ask, getting snippy. My irritation with myself and Noelle is rubbing off on how I'm interacting with him. "Sorry," I say. "I'm just...unsettled."

"I don't blame you," he says. "I saw the way she sort of swooped in and made sure Noelle was right there under her thumb."

"So, I'm not just imagining it?" I ask him, looking at him now.

"Not in the slightest," he says. His tone is dark. I don't like that.

I almost wish he'd told me that I *was* imagining it.

I look around the party. Hooper is still lost in

conversation with people that I assume are buddies of his from the high school he teaches at. Noelle is over in the corner with Jenna, talking to some other people who seem to be under Jenna's spell the same way Noelle is. The rest of the party rages on. It's loud, a cacophony of laughter and music. Finally, I've had enough and want to step outside.

"I think I need some air," I tell Cash.

"I'm right behind you," he says.

And the two of us head out onto the back patio.

Edison bulbs line the pergola that covers the patio. The warm glow casts romantic light on everyone gathered outside. There are groups of people here and there, and I spot two empty chairs on the far side of the patio, tucked back into a little area with lots of greenery around it. Cash and I would be pretty much hidden there. And there's a part of me that wants to disappear right about now.

I take a seat in the corner, somewhat obscured by the greenery around us. I'm not sure that anyone would know we were here unless they knew where to look. I like it that way. I'd prefer to just hide for the rest of the party and make a quick goodbye in about an hour or two. Then get the hell out of here. The fewer people I have to interact with until then, the better.

Cash takes the seat adjacent mine. The two chairs are facing a small table between them. I put my beer down on the glass table and adjust my shirt. After a moment, I realize Cash is staring at me. I look up at him.

"What?" I ask.

There's a softness in his gaze that makes my stomach flutter. I tug on my shirt some more even though I've adjusted it enough. I swipe my beer from the table and cross my arms in front of my chest.

"I'm just glad," he says with a crooked smile.

"Glad for what?" I ask.

"That you decided to work with me. In an official capacity," he says. "I wouldn't want to do it with anyone else, Blair," he adds.

"Are you sure about that?" I chuckle. "You have no idea what I'm like as an employee. In fact, I haven't been employed in a really long time. I might be *unemployable*, spoiled to the lifestyle I've become accustomed to. What if I'm difficult to work with?" I tease.

"This may come as a shock to you, but I'm already aware that you're difficult to work with," he says, shaking his head.

I laugh, feeling myself relaxing despite the urge to clench every muscle in my body tightly. Cash puts me at ease. He always has. Ever since I first met him. Even now, in this situation that I'd rather eat glass than be in, he's got me laughing, relaxing.

There's something to be said for that.

But there's also something to be said for the fact that men and women can be friends without sexual tension or romance coming into play. Aside from

Noelle, Cash is probably my closest friend. And right now, things aren't looking so good for Noelle and me.

Cash might be my best friend, I realize.

And the thought saddens me a little bit. There's still so much of myself that I keep hidden from him. Have I really become that closed off?

I guess I have.

But I feel like I had good reason. Your father disappearing will do that to you. Especially when it comes to trusting men ever again. Especially men who seem to be engaged in the same line of work that made your father vanish.

I clear my throat, my thoughts getting a little too heavy. I shift nervously in my seat, my anxiety returning.

"You alright?" he asks me, not for the first time tonight.

"I'm fine," I tell him, offering a smile that I hope seems more genuine than the one I handed him earlier.

Cash returns it, making me think it was convincing. I've gotten good at that. It's a skill I perfected over the last eight years. Eight years. God, has it already been another year since he disappeared? I guess so.

The thought makes me wonder if I should try to get in touch with Blake. But it's chased quickly by the sobering realization that a phone line works both ways, and Blake hasn't done anything to try and get in touch with me.

I'm all that's left of our family at this point, I

suppose. Blake doesn't really want anything to do with me. Dad's gone. Mom's been dead for thirty-plus years. No grandparents to speak of. No extended family. This is it.

The thought is heavy.

I feel it curling up on my chest like a cat, ready to settle in for a long winter's nap.

"Are you sure you're okay?" Cash asks. "You've been acting weird ever since you got into the truck."

His voice is enough to bring me back to the present and shake the heavy thoughts away from the forefront of my mind.

"I am, I promise," I tell him. "I guess I've just got a lot on my mind."

Not to mention I had a sex dream about you.

The thought makes me blush again. I take a big gulp of beer, hoping it'll wash the red away from my cheeks. The cool liquid is soothing going down my throat, the bite of its carbonation making me want to burp. I swipe at the corner of my mouth and let the beer rest on my thigh.

Cash starts to talk about the vampire series that we're working on. I tell him some of what I've found and that I'm going over my dad's book as a source. He's pleased with that. But it's midway through this conversation that I overhear another one. Just on the other side of where we're sitting. Obviously, someone thought they'd be alone out here.

"*Shhhh*," I motion with my finger for Cash to be quiet. He does.

The pair of us sit, alert and listening to a person on a phone call on the other side of the little garden area.

"Doesn't that freak you out, though?" the person on the call says.

There's a pause.

"It doesn't matter. I'm freaked out," he says. It's a guy. Maybe mid-thirties. I don't recognize his voice. A stranger to me, but someone that found their way onto the invitation list for Noelle's party.

The guy goes on, talking frantically into the receiver.

"I think I need to talk to Peter," he says.

I glance at Cash and one of his eyebrows arches at the name.

Peter. Jenna's ex-boyfriend.

"It might just be a coincidence, but who knows at this point? I'm worried. Wouldn't you be?" he asks.

There's silence for a while. Obviously, the person on the other end of the call is giving him an ear full.

"Don't tell me to calm down!" he hisses. Then he does seem to calm down slightly. "Listen. I'll talk to you later. I need to get a hold of Peter. Bye."

Then the guy walks around the corner of the house, and I recognize him.

He's older now. There are fine lines around his eyes. His hairline is receding a little bit. But I know him from my father's book. It's Nolan Jennings.

One of the people in the vampire roleplaying group.

CHAPTER ELEVEN

"OBVIOUSLY, he was talking about her boyfriend," I say as I shed my coat in the hallway back at my house. Cash follows suit, hanging his next to mine, and the two of us head into the living room where I left my little makeshift research station.

I plop down on the couch in my pile of blankets, and Cash sits down across from me.

"Could they suspect someone?" Cash asks me.

His face is serious, his brows knitted together. The implication is huge. The fact that Noelle could be right back in the middle of a murder investigation with Jenna at the heart of it isn't lost on me. And it's not lost on him, either.

"They would have to," I say. "Obviously not Peter. Why else would they want to involve him? That says to me that they think whoever the killer is, they're coming for one of them next. If it isn't Jenna, who is it?"

"According to your dad, Peter wanted nothing to do with Jenna after everything went down," Cash says. "But your dad always swore he could tell that Peter still cared about her. That he was still in love with her, even after everything she put him through."

"How romantic," I snark.

"Indeed," Cash says. "Romantic if you're into that whole Bonnie and Clyde sort of philosophy of love," he adds.

"Well, I'm not," I remark.

He snorts.

"Color me shocked," Cash says with a laugh.

"What's that supposed to mean?" I ask, smirking.

"I just can't imagine you giving an inch to anyone," he says.

"Good. I've given you the right impression," I say.

Cash laughs. And then there's a silent pause as if he's thinking.

"I think they were thinking about calling Peter because they had the same questions we do. Maybe they suspect Jenna herself. Or maybe they know something we don't," he adds.

The thought makes me wonder if I should have hung out longer. Should have made more of an effort to get Noelle alone. I didn't. But what would I have said?

Hey, do you think Jenna had anything to do with that murder they announced on the news today?

I don't know what I would have said to her.

The whole thing makes me feel powerless. And I

hate feeling that way. It's the same way I felt when my dad first went missing. Like there was nothing in the world I could do to make anything right again. I don't like the parallels that my subconscious is drawing between the two events right now. It's a slippery slope. One that I'm sure a therapist would have a lot to say about.

I think about what Cash said for a moment.

"If Jenna does have something to do with it, her motive would be to get back at everyone who avoided prison time, right?" I say. It's the only thing that makes sense. Why else would she risk her freedom?

"It's all I can come up with," Cash says. "It's too odd that this happened right after she got out of prison. It could have been her. Especially if she could find some time all to herself," he says.

He's not wrong. It's weird. Way weird.

The kind of weird that can't be chalked up to mere coincidence. The kind of weird that they end up making a documentary about years later.

Still, I can't imagine why she'd do that. Especially if she'd really gone to all the trouble to straighten things out with her family.

"Do you think Peter might know something?" I ask Cash.

He nods.

"I think if anyone does, it might be him. Especially if this is some elaborate plan," he adds.

An elaborate plan. I roll the idea over in my mind.

What would be the point of that? Proving to Jenna that he's still loyal to her after all this time?

Something about all of it isn't making sense.

But it's connected to Jenna.

I know that as well as the back of my own hand. There's no way this *isn't* connected to her in some way.

"Well, do you want to keep me company while I do some research?" I ask Cash.

"My laptop's in the car. I can help you," he says.

And while he jogs outside to get his stuff, I bury myself once again in my dad's book.

THE BEAUTIFUL AND THE DEAD
ANOTHER PIECE OF CORRESPONDENCE

To: g.graves@yahoo.com
From: mrdracula@yahoo.com
Subject: My first taste

As is the case with all young people—or most, I should say—the first time I tasted blood, it was my own. And it was an accident. An all-too-common occurrence for little boys, I bit my lip after crashing my bike and blood filled my mouth. I was alone in an alley just beyond the apartment complex where I grew up and I began to panic. The iron-laden taste burst on each of my taste buds, sending my brain into overdrive. I'd never tasted anything like it. And even then, I knew I wanted to taste it again.

And so I did. I began to cut myself at the age of ten, milking what little blood I could from my self-inflicted wounds. I would practice this nightly and my parents were none the wiser. It was when I turned thirteen that I got my first true taste of something Other.

There was a cat that lived outside our apartment complex. A raggedy old thing that had seen better days. So I set a trap for it. I dug a hole in the woods just beyond the complex. I rigged a broken part of a dog cage to fall down over the hole once the cat had slipped inside. I covered it with leaves and laid out treats for the cat. Within twenty-four hours, he was in my makeshift trap.

I drank from him. I killed him. And I knew then that I'd do it again and again if I needed to. But that was only my first victim. Not my first *human* victim.

I pored over the e-mail time and again, wondering if I was reading it right. If any of it was true or if I was just caught up in the ramblings of an attention-seeking vampire wannabe.

Despite my suspicion that this person might just be engaging in some heavy fantasy, there was something about the e-mail—and the series that would follow—that I found alarming. I'm not one to give in to ideas that one can detect honesty merely from the vibration that a person puts off, especially through text, but there was just something about the e-mail that rang true.

Like I really was reading this person's confession of the first time they'd drawn blood.

It was right around this time that I secured an interview with Peter Kilmer.

Yes, Peter Kilmer, the boyfriend of famed vampire would-be murderess, Jenna Prescott.

Peter told me that I could meet him at his dad's auto body shop, and I obliged, willing to take the interview wherever I could get it. If he'd told me to meet him at a vampire's den full of hungry revenants, I probably would have taken the invitation.

As it was, though, I met Peter in broad daylight, an unexpected turn of events. I thought that vampires mostly liked the nighttime. Daylight had been at his insistence, though.

When I arrived at the body shop, Peter was waiting outside. He was tall, lanky, and had long dark hair that fell past his shoulders. He looked like he belonged in a heavy metal band, not in a true crime volume. I waved at him as I got out of my car and headed up to meet him.

"Graham Graves," I told him, sticking out my hand to shake his.

He took it firmly, shaking my hand then running his hand through his hair as though he was very conscious of the image he put off. I could tell that he liked the idea of coming across as a little bit spooky. A little bit glamorous. But there was a heaviness to his eyes that made me wonder if the whole charade didn't bring him as much joy as it used to. I wondered if it was that appearance that had connected him with Jenna in the first place.

"Right this way," Peter said.

He led me to a table and chairs out back that looked like a place where the employees might take their breaks. There was a nervous air about him. I couldn't blame him. Here I was, a journalist (of sorts), come to talk to him about what was probably one of the most traumatic events in his short life. I would have been nervous, too.

Peter and I took seats across from each other at the small break table. The sounds of the auto body shop drifted out onto the little patio area, providing enough background noise that he seemed to relax a little bit. I wondered if he'd spent most of his life in this place, growing up beside his dad, watching him fix cars. The sounds probably provided him a degree of comfort.

Peter was young. At the time I interviewed him, only nineteen years old. Fresh out of high school, he was a kid. Despite that, he carried himself like an old man. Like someone that was bearing the weight of the world on their shoulders, and I couldn't help but believe it was because of what he went through with Jenna.

That was what I intended to find out.

I wanted to know anything and everything this kid would tell me about what had happened.

So, we began.

I asked him about his childhood, and he explained to me that it had been less than idyllic but hardly any worse than most people who wind up involved in the things he became involved in. His parents divorced when he was a child, his mother fleeing the marriage and moving halfway across the country, never to be seen again. His dad raised him. And while he didn't raise him with an iron fist, he did make sure to instill in Peter great American values such as not showing your emotions if you're a man. A value that too many of us have fallen victim to. It made it hard for Peter to be sure how his father felt about him.

And was likely one of the reasons he was so easily sucked into Jenna's game.

"It gave me a sense of belonging," he told me of the role-playing game. "And she had this presence that just made me feel seen," he went on. His eyes took on a glassy quality as he remembered her. "I'd never met anyone as beautiful as Jenna. You've seen her, haven't you?"

I was taken aback by the question. In my mind, these were a bunch of kids that got involved in something way over their heads. It never occurred to me that any of them were attractive. But he was right. Jenna was beautiful. And I could see how for a young man, her allure would have been strong. Especially a young man that craved attention from his parents.

"I have," I told him, of Jenna's looks. "I can understand why you would think she was beautiful."

"Not just beautiful, *gorgeous*. Like something out of a neoclassical painting," he corrected me.

I nodded, listening to the tale.

But there was something that struck me about it all. The telling of it. The way he referred to Jenna. There was no animosity in his voice for what she'd put him through. One thing was perfectly clear.

He was still in love with her.

And he probably would be for the rest of his life.

CHAPTER TWELVE

"CASH," I say, snapping the book shut. "We have to talk to Peter."

"Okay, I'm game for that," he says, looking up from his laptop.

"We just need to find him," I say.

"That shouldn't be too hard."

Cash clicks away on his keyboard. I sidle up next to him, very aware of how little space there is between the two of us. I can feel the heat radiating off his body, and I'm sure he can feel the same from me. I catch the scent of his cologne. It's faint, woodsy, masculine. I hate myself for noticing. I don't want to go down that path in my mind. Nothing good will come of it.

But then I think about him taking my hand.

It's all confusing. Maybe not confusing, but hard to navigate at the very least.

The last thing I want is to lose Cash as a friend.

But more than that, is there something I want? Desperately want?

I shut it down and clear my throat even though I haven't spoken any of it aloud. I resituate myself a little further away from Cash on the couch and look at his screen.

A Google search of Peter Kilmer gives us the basics and one of the first things to pop up is his Facebook page. Cash clicks on it.

I feel like I've stumbled onto a time capsule or stepped out of a time machine. Peter Kilmer looks exactly like he did in 1999. It's like he hasn't aged at all. His hair is still the same length. His skin is still just as pale and seems to have weathered the years really well. He doesn't look like he's in his forties.

One of the first things that Cash finds on the page is an event that Peter responded to, coming up this weekend. A goth dance night at one of Oklahoma City's few goth clubs.

"Well, I think you know what this means," Cash says.

I glance at him, unsure of where he's going with this.

"Get your fishnets ready. We're going to goth night."

AFTER HITTING up Hot Topic and a couple of thrift stores, I find my outfit for Friday night. I'm not proud of myself. Going in Hot Topic felt like another blast from the past. The store intimidated me as a teenager but going in as a thirty-something made me feel even weirder. But thirty bucks later, I had the fishnets that Cash instructed me to get.

I got a used leather jacket and a black tank top and skirt to go with them. I own a pair of combat boots, so that wasn't an issue. But when Friday night rolled around, makeup was. I watched at least five tutorials on how to do goth makeup before I picked up my brushes.

After about an hour of messing with it, I was pleased with what I saw in the mirror. Deeply smoked out eyes, winged eyeliner, and black lipstick. I look the part.

Standing in the hallway, I stare at myself in the mirror. The look is dramatic, and I simultaneously feel self-conscious and powerful. I have a feeling that where I'm going, I'll fit right in.

I sneak one last glance at my getup before I hear the sound of Cash's truck outside. I bounce out onto the porch and down the steps, then reach for the door handle of the passenger side door.

Cash whistles down at me when he sees me.

"Look at you!" he whoops.

I feel myself blush, surely visible even under all the foundation I have on.

"What do y'think?" I ask, doing a quick spin for him.

"Lookin' good," he says with a chuckle. But there's

something about it. Like something else is going unsaid. It makes it hard to breathe for just a split second. The implication of it. I'm probably just doing some wishful thinking.

I hop up into the truck, and before I shut the door, I take a look at what he's wearing and notice for the first time that he has a fishnet shirt on.

"Holy shit, you went all out," I say. The words come out before I get a chance to measure them in any way. My eyes are glued to the vision of his chest and abdomen through the fishnet. He looks like he stepped out of an ad for a goth dance night from the 90s.

"Too much?" he asks.

"No, no," I say, stumbling over my words. "Just enough," I say. I cringe immediately.

He chuckles again and then I shut the door. We're off.

"I thought dressing the part—really *committing* to it—might be fun," Cash says as he turns out onto the main road from my driveway. It's dark out, well past ten at night. The event starts at 10:30. We'll arrive just in time.

"It was a good idea," I tell him. "Even I have to admit that it was fun to get dressed up."

"Blair Graves admits to having fun. You heard it here first, folks," Cash remarks.

"Very funny," I say with a smile in my voice.

"I'll be here all week."

"What a treat."

I look over at him and see him smiling in the darkness. The expression does something funny to my stomach, making it flip flop in a way that I'm not sure it ever has upon noticing Cash smiling. Something's happening inside of me and I'm not sure that I like it. But I'm also not sure that there's any stopping it at this point. I sigh.

"You okay?" Cash asks after a beat.

"I'm fine," I tell him, a little too brightly.

We're back in that same cycle we were in the other night. Him asking me if I'm fine. Me lying and telling him that I am. Meanwhile, my mind is going places it shouldn't. His fishnet shirt doesn't help. Even if it's a tad ridiculous.

But Cash's eyes linger on me for a moment. What feels like a moment too long.

"You should probably watch the road," I tell him, then I smirk into the darkness.

CHAPTER THIRTEEN

THE CLUB IS in the heart of midtown. An area that's known for its hipster community and alternative artists sharing quadplexes next door to art galleries and strange boutiques. It's a wonderful part of town, in other words. I'm not shocked that the club we're going to is in the basement of one of these galleries.

Cash pulls up outside and finds parking across the street when someone leaving pulls out of their parking space. People walk back and forth along the sidewalk, some of them going into the art gallery and looking very much like they'll belong at the party in the basement. Others keep walking this way and that, going into the restaurant on one side and the late-night cafe on the other. I spot someone writing on a laptop in the window.

I unbuckle my seatbelt and sit there in the darkness of the truck for a moment as Cash parks and kills the engine. Nerves begin to take over. I tuck the seatbelt carefully back into its resting place, my sweaty palm sticking to the plastic. My heart beats faster in my chest. It occurs to me that we might be putting ourselves in danger.

"Do you think this is a good idea?" I ask Cash.

He looks at me.

"I'll keep you safe," he says.

He says it so matter-of-fact that it takes me aback. I'd never really thought about the fact that Cash *does* keep me safe wherever we go. And the reality is that most people aren't going to mess with a guy that's six and a half feet tall. I don't think I'd ever taken a moment to fully appreciate how safe that makes me feel.

"Thank you," I say sincerely.

There's something innocent and wholesome about the expression on his face, like he can't imagine a world where he wouldn't put my safety first. It makes the butterflies return to my stomach. I inhale sharply at the sensation.

"Ready?" he asks. Now he smirks.

"You're having too much fun with this," I tell him, returning the expression. I sigh. "I guess I'm as ready as I'll ever be."

"Let's go," he says.

I get out of the truck and follow him around to the sidewalk. A couple passes by, both dressed much like the two of us. I glance at Cash and half a smile curves his mouth. I find myself mirroring him.

"Come on," Cash says. He crooks his arm, and I take it, and he walks me into the gallery.

Music booms from below while soft tunes play up here. There's a sign pointing to the door that leads downstairs. There's a neon sign declaring that a club exists below our feet.

RAT'S NEST, it reads.

The name is just as intimidating as the people taking the stairs in front of us. The couple. They look like they could have stepped right out of a music video produced by Robert Smith. The big 80s goth hair and the clothes to match. Both have on fishnet, just like me and Cash. I guess he made a good call by demanding that I get some.

I feel the fishnets rubbing against each other as I take the dimly lit steps down into the basement club. The stairs twist and lead us further down, making me wonder what this place was originally. Maybe it was a speakeasy. That would make sense.

The idea gives the place a little bit more glamor. The idea that it's still a place where people come to get intoxicated and listen to music is kind of fun. As we make our way onto the bottom story landing, I see a neon frame with a piece of paper in it. I read it.

It declares that the Rat's Nest was the original name of the place, and like I thought, it was a speakeasy.

Built at the turn of the century, the Rat's Nest has always provided a place for society's outcasts. We continue that tradition by being one of Oklahoma City's oldest Goth clubs. We pride ourselves on being a place where all are welcome and weird is celebrated. Come, have a drink and make some magic.

I smile in the glowing aura of the sign. Pink neon stands out around the edges, lighting up the paper in the frame. Cash stands beside me, my arm still intertwined with his.

"Excuse me," a guy says from behind us.

"Sorry," Cash says, and steps around me, letting go of my arm. It makes me slightly sad. That brief skin to skin contact with him gone just like that. And as things are, I have no way of asking for it again. To do that, I'd have to come clean about how I feel about Cash.

And if I'm being honest with myself, I'm not sure *how* I'm feeling. I feel confused. I feel conflicted. But I like the way his skin feels against mine. I fear losing him if I make any move in that direction. It feels safer to stay in this hellish limbo. But there's a part of me that knows I can't stay here forever. Eventually, something will be a tipping point.

That scares the shit out of me.

All of this is racing through my mind as Cash steps up beside me. I feel myself flush with the thoughts. I take a deep breath.

"Everything alright?" he asks me.

"Fine," I tell him with a smile.

And honestly, it's the truth. There's probably nowhere I'd rather be than with him. The realization is dangerous. I beat it down, telling myself that there are plenty of other places I'd like to be right now. But I know the truth.

I'd go anywhere with Cash.

The thought is frightening. I can't remember the last time I felt like this about someone. All of my late twenties were spent recovering from the relationship I had in college. I sort of steeled myself against the possibility of falling for someone ever again. I knew it was stupid. I had this whole trajectory planned for myself. Grow old alone. I was okay with that.

Cash threw a wrench in all of that.

I smile up at him again, this time with a tinge of sadness.

How can we be two grown adults and not be able to tell each other how we feel? Of course, there's the possibility that he doesn't share my feelings at all. And that's what paralyzes me.

"Let's get a drink and go find somewhere to plant ourselves," he says.

"Sounds like a plan," I say, and he turns to step through the crowd. But then he turns back to look at me and he holds out a hand. I reach for it in the darkness, feeling his smooth, warm palm against mine. I let him pull me through the crowd, his giant frame snaking this way and that, parting the sea of people with his sheer size.

Finally, he pulls me up to the bar in front of him. He places his hands on either side of me. I can feel the warmth of his body behind me. My breath catches in my chest.

"Didn't want anyone to make you uncomfortable," he says into my ear. His breath is hot and for a moment I feel intoxicated even though I haven't had anything to drink yet. I turn, looking back at him. He smiles at me. It's almost enough to make me forget the whole reason we're here tonight.

I think again about how safe I am in his presence. And how I don't want that to ever end. I want him with me all the time.

It's the most honest I've been with myself about the whole situation.

It's terrifying.

Jesus. Get your shit together.

I swallow and look forward, meeting the bartender's eyes.

"Whiskey Coke with cherries," I tell him.

Cash gives him his order too and pulls out his card to pay when the bartender returns with our drinks.

"It's the least I can do for dragging you out here tonight," he tells me.

Cash hands me my whiskey Coke and he takes his plain whiskey. He holds up his glass to mine.

"Cheers," he says.

"To what?" I ask.

"To us," he says.

The statement makes my stomach flutter.

"We make a good team, don't we?" he asks.

"We do," I say, almost breathless.

He clinks his glass with mine and takes a sip. I follow suit and take the first sip of my whiskey Coke, savoring the flavor of Coca-Cola and Jack Daniels mixing together on top of my palette.

I swallow. It burns slightly and I feel the alcohol start to run through my veins. I make a mental note not to drink too much, though I don't think Cash would let me in light of why we're here in the first place.

We're looking for Peter.

"I see a table," Cash says into my ear above the sounds of music throbbing throughout the club. He holds out his hand again and I take it. He leads me across the dance floor to the table he spotted. We both grab a seat. It's a two top, so there's no danger of anyone else sitting with us, and we have a great view of the club. In the neon lights, it should be easy to pick Peter out if he really does come tonight.

Cash and I both cast glances around the room, trying to seem as casual as possible.

I watch people moving, limber and fluid, on the dance floor. Alcohol is flowing and everyone seems to have arrived. The place is getting packed, and I keep my eyes on the entrance, feeling like Peter could show up at any minute, but I don't spot him. Instead, my focus lands on a girl that has her eye on Cash. I feel unwanted jealousy flare in my chest, but when I look at Cash, he seems oblivious.

I turn my attention back to trying to find Peter but to no avail. He's nowhere to be found. But just then, Cash reaches across the table, grabbing my arm.

Over the din of the busy bar, he speaks.

"Blair!" I hear my name above the sounds around us.

I snap my head to look at Cash and I follow his gaze.

And there, standing on the far end of the bar, is the man of the hour.

Peter Kilmer.

"LET'S GO," Cash says into my ear after standing up and coming around to my side of the table.

I stand up and shove my chair back in. Cash is already heading across the dance floor. I jog to catch up with him, his much longer strides giving him quite the advantage.

We cut through the dancers and at one point I lose him, bodies pressing up against my own and making me claustrophobic. I feel the heat from them and the movements of the dance going on around me. Suddenly, I feel like I can't breathe that well. I push forward, knowing that salvation is waiting for me on the other side of the dance floor. And seconds later, I emerge from the crowd and look for Cash.

I spot his giant frame instantly. He hulks over the people around him, and he's narrowing in on Peter. Peter stands at the end of the bar, sipping on a cocktail. A woman drapes herself over him at his side. The look on his face makes me think the advance is unwanted. Or at the very least, he's indifferent to her.

Cash casts a glance back at me and stops in his tracks just before we get up to Peter.

"You do the talking," I tell him.

Cash nods, apparently having planned on that from the beginning.

I follow as he takes the lead and heads over to where Peter stands. He clears his throat, and the sound is barely audible above the music, even though Cash makes a big deal of it and tries to do it as loudly as he can. However, Peter seems eager for the interruption and looks away from the woman beside him, focusing his attention on the man in front of him.

"Hey, sorry to interrupt," Cash says.

The woman standing next to Peter looks annoyed. Her mouth twists slightly, making me think that we're doing a good job of ruining her night. I offer her a pressed smile, feeling slightly embarrassed. She doesn't return it.

She turns her focus back to Cash. I wonder if she's going to say something, but she remains quiet.

"Are you Peter Kilmer?" Cash asks Peter.

Peter's eyes narrow slightly. It's a microexpression, only there for a fleeting moment.

"I am," Peter says slowly. "What's this about?"

"My colleague and I were just wondering if we could talk to you for a little while," Cash says.

Peter casts a glance at me. His eyes rove over my body and when he looks me in the eye, it's apparent that he weighed me, judged me, and found me wanting. I want to tell him whatever went through his mind was never on the table to begin with and not to flatter himself.

I shift my weight and cross my arms, feeling hostile.

I tell myself to tamp it down. It's probably not the right moment to take a feminist stand. Or at least it's not worth it. We just want information out of Peter, and my ultimate goal is to find out if Noelle is safe. That's the whole reason we're here tonight.

Peter casts a glance at the woman standing next to him, almost like he's considering using her as an out. Ultimately, he doesn't. He steps away from her toward me and Cash.

"We can talk," Peter says. "Why don't we go outside?"

Cash nods and looks at me as if for approval. I swallow and nod slowly, not especially keen on the idea of leaving the club with Peter. We have no idea if he had anything to do with the recent murder. And here we are, neither of us detectives, neither of us armed, going out into an alley with Peter Kilmer. One of Jenna Prescott's most intimate associates.

Cash must see the fear in my eyes. He reaches down and squeezes my hand once when Peter turns to lead us out of the club. I follow Cash up the stairs and Peter heads for the back of the art gallery, headed for the alley, just like I feared.

But when we emerge outside, there's a patio with a handful of people sitting or standing, sipping on drinks and discussing the art they saw in the gallery tonight. A few of them look like goths that are taking a break from the loud, dark club.

Peter finds us a table in the corner, away from everyone.

"Let me guess," Peter says with a sigh as he sits down. He spreads out, his legs going out in either direction. He's not uncomfortable. That much is apparent. "You want to talk about Jenna."

Cash raises an eyebrow, clearly surprised at Peter's directness.

I remain silent.

"Yeah," Cash says.

"I figured. You look familiar," Peter says to Cash. "You a journalist?"

"Not exactly," Cash says. "I run a YouTube channel."

"Fair enough," Peter says. "What do you want to know?"

Cash clears his throat, clearly unprepared for Peter to be so open and willing to talk about things.

"Well, I'm sure you know that Jenna's out of

prison," Cash begins. "I was wondering if you'd seen her or had any contact with her since then."

"I haven't heard from or seen Jenna in years," Peter says. But something about his tone is sad. Like he wishes that wasn't the case. "I'm pretty sure she doesn't want to hear from me."

"But you want to hear from her?" Cash asks.

"Not necessarily," Peter says. "It's probably for the best that we stay away from each other. But I miss her, that's for certain."

"Do you still have feelings for her?" Cash asks.

"Have you ever met someone and known they were going to change the course of your life? For better or worse, you just laid eyes on them and knew that this was *it*. This was your *person*. That you'd do anything for them?" Peter asks.

Cash clears his throat, shifting uncomfortably in his seat. My body stills beside him. I know exactly what Peter's talking about, I'm afraid. And it makes my breath catch in my chest.

"I do," Cash finally says. It seems like it takes him forever to say it. Peter glances from Cash to me with a look of understanding. I blush furiously, hoping that no one can see it out here in the dim patio light.

Cash clears his throat, and I shift around nervously.

"That's how I felt about her," Peter says. "I'd never met anyone like her. And I knew—even then—that I'd never meet anyone like her ever again in my life. For better or worse."

"That's quite a realization to have at such a young age," I remark.

"When you know, you know, right?" Peter says with a sad smile.

"So, I'm sure you've seen the news recently," Cash says.

"Actually, I don't keep up with it," Peter counters.

Cash glances at me.

I clear my throat now.

How am I supposed to tell this guy that the reason we're questioning him is that we think he might have had a hand in what I'm about to tell him took place just nights before?

We're basically accusing him of being an accomplice to murder.

Or at the very least dredging up things I'm sure he'd rather not think about, particularly if he's innocent. I suddenly feel guilty. Embarrassed. But I press forward, reminding myself that my main motivation for being here tonight is to find out how safe Noelle is right now.

"Someone was killed," I say. I struggle for the words and glance at Cash. He takes over.

"And the style of the killing was vampiric in nature," Cash says.

Peter laughs.

"Oh, I see," he says.

I blush.

"We just wondered if you'd heard anything about it," Cash says.

"Look," Peter says. "I haven't run in those circles in a really long time. I wouldn't even begin to know the first thing about any of it."

"So, you don't think Jenna would have had anything to do with it?" I ask, feeling hopeful for the first time about the whole situation.

"I doubt it," Peter says. "I can't imagine she'd do something like that right after being free for the first time in over two decades. Besides, what would her motive be? She had her reasons for wanting to kill her stepfather," Peter goes on. "She never enlightened me as to what they were, but I knew her motivation was strong."

"She never told you why?" Cash asks, sounding bewildered. I don't blame him. I feel the same way.

But then I think about what he just told us about the way he felt when he first met Jenna. You'd do anything for someone you felt so deeply for. And Peter very nearly did.

"No," Peter says. "She almost did once but decided not to. Who doesn't hate the guy that replaced their dad, though? Especially when your mom was cheating with your new stepdad before she was divorced from your dad. 'You're either with me or you're not,' she'd said. And I was with her. Right up until I wasn't." A bitter smile curves his mouth. "I was a coward for not helping her."

The statement takes me aback.

That he would feel that way, especially after all this time, makes my stomach feel funny. And not in a good, fun butterfly kind of way. More like existential dread. And the knowledge that this guy would prob-ably still do anything for Jenna. I swallow, feeling suddenly very aware of myself in his presence and wishing I was back at home, snug under the covers in my bed.

Cash nods.

"Would you still kill for her?" Cash asks.

I gasp slightly at the question and wish instantly that he hadn't asked it. My eyes go wide, and I look at Peter, and he's smiling at Cash in the darkness.

"I don't know," Peter says. "And if I did, why would I tell you?" he adds.

I feel unsettled. I want Cash to finish this up. I want to go home. I go silent, hoping that even the sound of my breathing isn't audible. I want to disap-pear. Suddenly, this all feels far more dangerous than it did originally.

This guy would kill for her. Still. I can see it plainly on his face.

"I guess that's all we wanted to know," Cash says. There's a steely edge to his voice. I have to fight the urge to reach out and grab his arm, tell him to stop. Instead, I sit there quietly, motionless.

"Well, if that's all you need, I'll be getting back to the party," Peter says, standing up.

And then he walks away, leaving me and Cash sitting there together at the little bistro table.

"Well," Cash says. "That didn't sit well with me."

"I think we should go," I tell him.

And he nods.

The two of us get up and head back through the gallery out to his truck. And I heave a deep sigh of relief once the door shuts and I hear the lock click into place. I look at Cash in the darkness.

"I think maybe Peter has something to do with this," I tell him.

He turns his ignition and looks at me, illuminated by the green of the dash.

"I think you may be right," he says.

And it does nothing to calm the unsettled feeling radiating throughout my body.

CHAPTER FOURTEEN

CASH and I ride in silence all the way back to the house. The drive seems to stretch on longer than it should. The heaviness of the conversation with Peter hangs over us like a wet blanket. Any fun we were having on the way to the club seems long gone. Now I just feel out of place in my ridiculous outfit, and I'm sure Cash feels the same way.

He pulls up out front of the Solomon House and I unbuckle my seatbelt.

"Do you want to come in?" I ask him.

He nods his head silently. The pair of us get out of the truck and I unlock the door, letting him into the house. I head down the long entry hall and call back to him over my shoulder.

"Want anything to drink?" I ask.

"Something strong," Cash replies.

"Best I can do is beer tonight," I tell him with a chuckle.

"That works," he calls back to me.

I grab two Coors Lights out of the fridge and meet him in the living room. Both of us clad in fishnet, looking like we stepped out of a music video for a 90s goth band.

Cash takes a seat on one side of the couch, and I hand him his beer.

"Thanks," he says.

He cracks it open, and I do the same with mine, taking a long swig and thinking that it's going to take more than one beer to calm my nerves tonight. All I can think about is how Noelle might be in danger. All that keeps running through my mind is the way that Peter acted about Jenna, and how he wished he'd finished the job he'd started years ago.

It's a pretty dark revelation.

My mind skips back for a moment to when Cash told Peter that he knew what it was like to meet someone like that. Unbidden, jealousy flares in my chest. The idea that he could feel that way about someone hits me like a freight train. Along with the idea that whoever he felt that way about, it wasn't me.

The dread I'd been feeling is replaced by something else. Something emptier.

I try to shake it off, reminding myself that the whole reason I went out tonight was to make sure

Noelle was okay. And even though I didn't accomplish that, I need to cling to the idea. I don't want to feel the other emotions that are bubbling just below the surface.

I take a seat on the opposite side of the couch and take another long drink.

"Well," I say. "I don't know that we found out what we wanted to."

"I don't know about that," Cash says. "I think we got a pretty compelling argument for the idea that Peter might still be involved with Jenna. Regardless of what he says. And even if he's not right now, it was clear that if she gave him half a chance, he'd help her."

"Make things right," I murmur.

"Exactly," Cash says.

"Crazy," I mutter.

"What's crazy?" he asks.

"Just the idea that after all this time, he'd still put his life on the line for her. His freedom, I mean," I say. "You saw the way his face changed when he talked about her. Like this bittersweet expression. I think there's a part of him that still thinks there's a chance they could end up together."

"Hell, he might not be wrong," Cash says. "I could see her getting back with him if she thought she could count on his loyalty. And exploit his guilt to get it."

I nod. I *could* see that.

Jenna is nothing if not an opportunist. And I can completely imagine her exploiting any guilt that Peter might feel about how things went down back in the day.

I'm silent for a moment.

"He did bring up one thing, though, that keeps sticking in my mind," I say.

"What's that?"

"What the hell would her motive be if she killed that guy?" I ask.

"Old crony being put in their place?" Cash poses.

"So, basically, she wants revenge for the fact that no one else paid for the crime? Even though really the only people involved were her, Peter, and Noelle?" I ask.

"That's my thought," Cash says. "I mean, she's the only person connected to the crime that has a felony record," he adds.

I make a non-committal noise.

He's probably right. The thought is haunting. The idea that she could be wrapped up in this and therefore be putting Noelle at risk. Or worse, what if Noelle is next?

I shake my head.

"What's wrong?"

"I just had a dark thought," I tell Cash.

"Which was?" He raises an eyebrow.

"What if this is just the beginning?" I ask. "What if she wants revenge on everyone that was involved? Especially the person whose testimony put her away."

A shocked realization washes over Cash's features.

"Shit," he mutters.

"Exactly," I say. I chug the rest of my beer and burp. "Want another one?" I ask.

Cash chugs the rest of his, apparently being hit by the same urge that I am. The seriousness of the situation seems to be washing over both of us. This might only be the beginning. He nods and hands me his empty can. I stand up and start heading for the kitchen, then turn to face him.

"Do you think you should call that detective?" I ask him.

"I think that's probably a good idea," he says. "I'll be right back."

He gets up and heads for the back patio, digging his phone out of his pocket. I head for the fridge and grab both of us another beer. I crack both cans open and head back for the living room, alone with my own thoughts for a moment.

What if Jenna *is* involved in all of this?

How the hell do I bring this up with Noelle?

What if someone else ends up getting killed?

Cash is outside for a few minutes and finally comes back in. He sighs as he shuts the patio door.

That's not a good sign.

"Well?" I ask.

"They don't seem to be concerned," Cash says, frustration written on his features.

I sigh, equally frustrated.

That's the last thing I wanted to hear. I want to tell

them this is important. It makes me feel helpless. Like a child before the whole thing. Like there's nothing I can do to make Noelle safer. And I wish that there was. That's all I want to do in this situation.

I feel the desire to reach out to her. Tell her that she can't hang out with Jenna anymore. It would be useless. I know how she'll respond to that. No one wants their best friend to tell them they're fucking up. But Noelle *is* fucking up. And I'd be a bad friend if I didn't tell her that.

I sigh again and bring my hands to my face, rubbing it hard. I wish I could just go to sleep tonight and wake up tomorrow and none of this be happening.

But I know it doesn't work that way.

"So, what now?" I ask Cash.

He looks up at me, his face still cast downward at his phone.

"Well," he says. "We could just leave it all alone," he says. "Or we could keep digging."

As I look at him, I already know which answer we're going with. The second one.

"You know I can't leave this alone," I tell him.

"I know," he says. "I completely understand. Hopefully, if we're lucky, this will be it. Just the one murder. Random. Not involving Jenna or anyone she knows."

"Hopefully," I say.

Though I don't feel hopeful.

Not a little.

Not at all.

. . .

AFTER CASH and I kill a couple more beers a piece, I suggest that we turn something on the television. I also tell him that I don't know how late he wants to stay up, but I'm going to need to get into something more comfortable than fishnets.

"Understood," he says with a chuckle.

"Are you sure you're okay in that?" I point at his shirt.

"Actually, it itches," he tells me.

"You can take it off," I tell him.

He looks at me, almost like he's making sure that I really said that. I nod, dispelling any notion that he has that I didn't say it.

"Go for it," I say.

I disappear around the corner and head upstairs for my bedroom. I slip out of my get up for the night and find some pajama pants. I grab a slouchy gray t-shirt that hangs off my shoulder and return downstairs, leaving the light beside my bed on.

It's always nice to go into a bedroom that's inviting. And having some warm light coming from the far side of the bed always does that for me.

I round the corner of the living room and stop dead in my tracks.

I told him he could take his shirt off.

But I wasn't really prepared for it.

Cash sits, his perfectly chiseled chest and abdomen

out for all the world to see. His fishnet shirt cast onto the coffee table. I blink once, twice, three times. He looks up at me.

"I can put it...uh...back on," he says, then clears his throat. But I notice, as he does, he glances at my bare shoulder. I reach for the fabric of my shirt and pull it back up to cover myself. I swallow, my throat feeling thick and it's hard to find my voice when I speak.

"No, it's great," I say. "I mean, it's fine."

Cash shifts in his seat, looking nervous. I want to tell him he can't be as nervous as I am. Part of me wants to walk right over and climb across his lap and just kiss him. Another part of me is terrified at how he'd react. Still another part is chastising the part that wants to climb him like a tree.

I clear my throat and grab the remote off the end table and resituate myself back on my side of the couch.

I focus my eyes on the television, telling myself not to look at Cash, even though I want to. But as I scroll through the available streaming services, I would swear that I can see that Cash is looking at me. I glance over and sure enough, he's staring. He looks away quickly and my eyes stray over his body.

I look back at the television.

I find a documentary for us to watch. This one's about Bigfoot. There will probably be little that either of us don't know, but there's something comforting about having him here. I don't want him to leave.

"Do you want a blanket?" I ask him.

"Yeah, actually," he says.

I reach for the blanket that's usually on this end of the couch. But the only blanket that's here is the one that's currently over my lap.

"You can have this one," I say, pulling it off my legs.

"No, keep it," he says. "I don't want to take your blanket."

"Take it," I tell him. "I'm fine."

"We could share it," he ventures. There's something cautious about the way he says it. Like he'd been rolling the idea over in his mind long before he spoke it.

"Oh, uh, yeah," I say.

I swallow. Suddenly I'm aware of every nerve ending on my body. I feel the way my shirt hangs off my shoulder. And I crawl over to his end of the couch, blanket in tow.

I scoot up next to him, allowing enough space between us so that we're not touching. I hand him the blanket. With his long arms, he spreads it out over both of us. He pulls it up over his chest and I do the same. The documentary plays in the background. It occurs to me that this is the closest we've ever been to each other.

My heart pounds in my chest, the sound of it threatening to echo throughout the room around us. I wonder if he can hear it. I wonder if he can feel it, reverberating in the air between us. It's too loud. I swallow, my mouth having suddenly gone dry.

Cash clears his throat and shifts a little in his seat.

He inches closer to me. I can feel the heat from his body growing more intense. I could reach out right now and place a hand on his chest. I want to do that. I *can't* do that.

Can I?

Out of the corner of my eye, I catch movement. For a split second, I'm scared to look. But I react more quickly than I can stop. Cash stares at me. His eyes dart to my mouth. Back to my eyes. He inhales sharply.

I feel my own breath still in my chest.

"I...uh..." Cash starts to speak. I can feel his breath on my face.

"Yeah," I say, the word out of my mouth before I can stop it.

Cash stretches out an arm and wraps it around me. Without another word, he pulls me up close to him. He places a kiss on the top of my head and my body relaxes against his. Neither of us say anything. And neither of us will likely acknowledge this tomorrow. But right now, it's happening. And I'm happy.

CHAPTER FIFTEEN

I WAKE IN THE NIGHT. The television rests on the home screen, lighting up the living room in a too-bright blue. I stretch and suddenly realize that I'm alone. The place where Cash had been sitting, cuddled beside me, is empty. I reach out a hand, feeling the cushion of the couch next to me.

It's cold.

I look at my phone, check the time. It's past four in the morning.

I spot a sticky note on the coffee table and lean forward to grab it, groaning as I do so. I'm not used to sleeping sitting up.

Had to go. Talk tomorrow. -C

I'm left with a hollow feeling as I read the words. I think about all the times my dad had to leave town unexpectedly. I think about how close I feel with Cash and how I hate that there's something fragile about the connection. Like I know that either of us can only get so close. I know that Cash has his own demons. His own secrets.

But there's something about us. When we're together, everything makes sense for me. And I haven't had that in a really long time. Maybe ever.

No one has ever made me feel safe the way he does.

The thought fills my heart with an ache. It's bittersweet.

I go into the kitchen and put on some coffee, even though it's prior to the crack of dawn. I might as well get started early. I can have a nap later. And besides, I'm not going to be able to fall back asleep anyway.

I stand in the kitchen, waiting for the caffeine fix. The smell of coffee fills the kitchen and the hallway, the whole first floor of the house. There's something about it that's comforting. I think it's because my dad would make coffee at all hours of the day. Smelling it would let me know I wasn't alone in the house.

It's something I haven't thought about in some time. Maybe something I haven't allowed myself to think of in a long time.

There's a part of me that wants to send Cash a text. Ask him where he went. There's a part of me that wishes he was still here, asleep next to me. I wonder if he ever actually fell asleep. I wonder if I snored.

Suddenly, I'm filled with anxiety that I don't want or need. I sigh.

This is one of the reasons I don't want to go down that road with him.

Things are good the way they are. Why fuck that up?

Because you're good at that.

I take a deep breath.

It's true that I haven't really had a relationship with a man since college. I've dated guys here and there, and I've sabotaged it at every turn. But I've never had anything quite like *this*.

There's something about Cash that's special. There's something about the way he makes me feel safe. Not just physically, but safe to be myself around him. It's rare. Especially as an adult, after the world has beaten you down as well as it can.

It's hard to find someone that you can let the walls down with.

If we pursued anything romantic, it could totally change that dynamic. It could ruin it.

Besides, I'm not even sure how he feels.

With that in mind, I do another thing that I do well: I bury it. I bury it in research and crack open my dad's book for another chapter.

THE BEAUTIFUL AND THE DEAD
I HEAR FROM MY PEN PAL AGAIN

Quite some time passed before my next correspondence with my mysterious self-identified vampire. I checked my e-mail late one night after getting home from the radio station, and I was greeted with this.

To: g.graves@yahoo.com

From: mrdracula@yahoo.com

Subject: A taste of man

I forbid myself from drinking from another living thing after my experience with the cat. I promised myself that I wouldn't let my taste for blood get the better of me. I continued to cut myself and drink my own blood. I even sucked the blood from raw meat when I could. I attempted to get pig's blood from a local butcher but it was hard to come by and they got suspicious after I came back the third time.

I was able to stave off my thirst for years. But it was when I was a teenager that I could no longer.

I got a fake ID and I started going to bars, looking for someone that might not expect to meet a vampire but who would be willing if they did. I didn't dress the part. I looked normal. I would stay until last call, remaining sober as the people around me grew more and more intoxicated. I did this for months without finding the perfect victim, but finally, one spring night, I found him.

A young man, about my age, was sitting in the corner of the bar, clearly alone. And very clearly intoxicated beyond the point of being able to get himself home. You'll probably think me a monster for what I'm going to tell you next, but I'm just relaying to you my experience and what I had to do to satiate my natural thirst. I view myself as nothing more than an animal—a predator—and therefore, beyond the rules of human morality.

This boy was beautiful. I've never considered myself homosexual, but many of those that I've fed on have been men. I don't discriminate with my victims. There is something unique about the taste of each of them. I'm able to tell things about their genetics, their diet, how hydrated they are, among other things. But there was something about this boy, as I drew closer, that was particularly sweet-smelling. And I would later learn that it was his desperation.

He greeted me eagerly when I approached his table. He even propositioned me, telling me that he'd do whatever I wanted for fifty dollars. I smiled and told him I wasn't interested in paying him. He seemed shocked at that. It was like he couldn't compute the idea that someone would be interested in him for anything other than sex. Especially not sex that wasn't trans-actional.

I talked to him for a while, trying my best to put him at ease with me. I wanted it to be easy. I didn't want him to fight me, and the more I got to know him, the more I realized just how easy it would be. He was seeking valida-tion, approval, and he didn't care where it came from or what he had to do to get it.

I suggested we leave and he came with me. I took him to my car and told him I wanted to take him somewhere special. I drove him out to a spot that was notorious for hook ups. A lake just outside of the city that the cops seemed to ignore because it was such a rough area. The people who went there were the dregs of society, in their eyes, which served my purposes well.

He seemed unphased by the location. It made me wonder if it was somewhere he'd been before. Perhaps even somewhere he'd been often. Maybe with others who had paid him to be there. He made no indication other than his complete nonchalance about being there. I parked the car near the water and we talked some more. Finally, I stretched my arm out behind him and we locked eyes. I leaned over and he leaned in, anticipating that I was going to kiss him. But just as our mouths were about to meet, I tilted his head to the side, revealing the side of his white neck.

He made no sound as I pressed my mouth to the side of his throat, surely thinking that my intention was to kiss him there. And for a brief second, I did. But then I bit down.

In myth, legend, and Hollywood, vampires have fangs that extend far beyond the normal canines of a human. In reality, that's not the case, and the force of a bite that will break the skin is extreme. He cried out as I clamped down on him with my jaws. I brought another hand up to silence him. He fought me only for a moment and then I tasted the sweetness of his life force.

His blood flowed eagerly into my mouth.

Almost like his body was begging me to drain him. He relaxed against me, as if put under some spell by my bite. It was intoxicating. More-so than any sexual encounter had ever been in my young life. I savored it, sucking on him and tasting him, wanting more of him. I wanted to entirely consume him. Make him a part of me forever. And I knew that, in a way, he would be.

I didn't kill him.

When I finished feeding from him, I felt more alive than I ever had in my life. I kicked him out of the car and he collapsed on the dirt beside the vehicle. I was through with him and tossed him out like discarded food waste, which is what he was to me. He cried out, weakened from my feeding. He reached out a hand, begging me not to leave him there. But I did.

I drove off into the night, my heart pounding wildly, knowing that this marked a moment in my life from which there would be no possible return. I had become something else entirely.

I had become a true vampire.

I stared at the e-mail. My computer was the only light in the room and I'm sure my face was a gaunt mask of abject horror in that lighting. I felt like I'd just read a confession. Even though he hadn't admitted to murdering the boy, it was clear that he had assaulted him, at the least. I wondered instantly what had happened to the boy.

I read it again. Then a third time, making sure that what I was seeing was what had been sent to me. It had been his intention to shock, I thought. There was a good chance that none of this was true. Like I'd origi-nally thought, this person was likely given to great fantasy, and this was an exercise in that. Perhaps there was some kind of sexual gratification for him in sharing these experiences. A way to relive it. Almost like a serial killer.

The thought chilled me.

If this wasn't just an exercise in sexual fantasy, it might have actually happened.

And there was no way to really tell if this guy had ended the encounter where he said he had.

I immediately shot off an e-mail to a contact of mine at the library. I asked them to dig up any crime articles they could find that fit the time frame of the encounter. I wanted to know if anything had been reported. But it was the middle of the night and there was a next to zero chance that my contact was checking his e-mail.

Which meant that I went to bed that night with visions of vampires dancing through my head.

CHAPTER SIXTEEN

BY ABOUT NOON, I'm yawning and desperately ready for some rest. I place a bookmark in my dad's tome on vampires and snuggle down on the couch with the plush blanket that's been over my lap all morning. I grab my phone to check it—really to check for a message from Cash I might have missed—but there are no new notifications. I lock my phone and reach above my head to lay it on the arm of the couch.

My hand pats and searches the end table for the remote. I find it and turn on the television. On the local channels, daytime TV is raging. Soap operas and talk shows. There isn't much better on the cable channels. Most of it programming for kids or non-prime time media, none of it anything that holds my interest for more than a few seconds. Finally, I take it back to one of the local channels just as the noon news broadcast is starting.

I place the remote back on the end table and then tuck both my hands under the covers, pulling them up to my chin. I just want the noise of the broadcast in the background. I have no intention of watching it. I only halfway listen to the beginning of it, but then something catches my attention and my eyes shoot open.

"We have a breaking news story in Oklahoma City," the anchor says. She's a pretty young girl. Younger than you'd think a news anchor should be. It's probably a sign that I'm nearing middle age—the fact that so many people in positions of power seem way too young to be there. "Another body has been found near Lake Draper, bringing to mind the idea that this killing could be connected to another body that was found only days ago in the same location. Emerging details of both cases seem to align, giving residents near the lake reason for concern. It should also be noted that both persons found at the lake were connected to a 1999 attempted homicide case involving Jenna Prescott, who was recently released from prison. This time, the male victim was Travis James."

I sit up.

Suddenly, all of the sleepiness I was feeling evaporates into nothingness. My heart thuds in my chest and I can feel my pulse throughout my body. My palms sweat and my skin grows clammy.

This is the first time that anyone has publicly made the connection between the recent murders and Jenna. This means that Noelle would absolutely have to be sticking her head in the sand like an ostrich to avoid this little nugget of information.

This means that there's a good chance that she's in danger. Which means that I would be a poor excuse for a friend—let alone a *best* friend—if I don't say something to her, no matter how she reacts.

I sit there, shocked and numb after my initial reaction. I'm exhausted, but I know this needs to be dealt with. I grab my phone and do the next logical thing.

I call Cash.

FIVE RAPID KNOCKS at the door announce that my visitor is here. I hop off the couch and jog down the hallway to the door. I grab the handle and throw it open.

"Come in," I say.

Cash passes me and heads for the living room, where our makeshift research station is still set up. He has his laptop tucked under his arm along with a legal pad. He's ready to work. I close the door and have to walk quickly to catch up with him. I round the corner, and he sits down on the couch, opening his laptop on his lap.

"You think it's already up on social media?" he asks.

"I haven't checked, but probably," I say. "Don't they stream the broadcasts?"

"Looking now," Cash says. With a few clicks he navigates to the local news station's Facebook page.

I walk around behind the couch so I can watch over his shoulder. And then he finds it.

"That's it," I point to the screen.

Cash clicks on it and we watch it. Me for the second time, him for the first. Both of us remain silent as the anchor relays the information that caused me to call Cash and tell him he needed to come over in the first place.

When it ends, we stay silent for a few moments. Finally, Cash speaks.

"Have you talked to Noelle yet?" he asks.

I knew he'd ask. I'd been dreading it. Almost as much as I'm dreading the actual conversation with her. I sigh.

"Not yet," I say.

Cash is quiet for a moment.

"You have to," he says.

"I know," I say, my tone defensive. "Sorry."

"I get it," Cash says. "It's never fun to tell someone they're fucking their life up. No one ever wants to hear that. Even from a trusted source. Maybe *especially* from a trusted source."

"Right?"

Cash grunts and closes his laptop.

"So what do we do now?" I ask him.

He rubs the stubble on his chin and then rubs the back of his neck like he's thinking hard.

"I think...we go check it out tonight," he looks back at me. There's a question in his statement. He's asking me, not so much telling me. I stand up and back away slightly.

"Are you sure that's a good idea?" I ask.

"I think it's a good way to find out a little bit more information," Cash says.

It occurs to me how dangerous that could be. Cash must read it on my face.

"If anything is weird, we leave," he assures me. "And besides, I don't think whoever it is will dump another body tonight. That would be too soon," he says.

I roll this over in my mind. He has a point. They probably wouldn't do that. Don't they need a cooling off period between murders if they're a serial killer?

But serial killers often choose random victims. Not ones that are connected. What if this person is open to operating on opportunity? They could have another one tonight and we might end up in the middle of it. I bite my lip.

"It'll be okay, Blair," Cash says. "I won't let anything happen to you."

He reaches for my hand and I give it to him. He rubs his thumb over my knuckles. I feel a surge of something—affection?—and then I pull away, afraid of the emotions it's awakening in me. I don't want to have to talk myself down right now. I'm already on edge from the news story and the fact that I'm going to have to say something to Noelle about the whole thing.

I sigh.

In a way, going out there tonight would be my way of trying to protect her. And I can't deny that there's a part of me that wants to know the truth. I look at Cash. His eyes are almost pleading.

"Okay, fine," I say.

He smiles at me, clearly glad that I've acquiesced to his desires. I can't help but smile back at him, even though I'm a little bit annoyed.

Not just annoyed—scared.

I try to hide that, though, when I look at him. I'm filled with a warmth at the idea that Cash has every intention of keeping me safe. And he's huge. I can't imagine someone looking at him and thinking it would be a good idea to piss him off. Only a crazy person would do that.

But then another thought occurs to me: only a crazy person would drain a murder victim of blood and make it look like a vampire got them.

So, maybe we're dealing with someone who *is* crazy.

The thought isn't comforting.

But here we are, and this is my life now.

CHAPTER SEVENTEEN

CASH LEAVES in the middle of the afternoon to run some errands. I briefly think about asking to go with him, but the thought occurs to me that I still need to call Noelle and ask her if she's aware of what's going on. Ultimately, if this person is killing people connected to Jenna, Noelle is in imminent danger. I dread how she's going to react, though. I can't imagine it's going to be good or go the way I want it to. I know how this sort of thing works. I think about prefacing my warning with *Don't shoot the messenger, Noelle.*

I'm not sure that it's going to do much good, though.

I take a deep breath and grab my phone. I shoot off a text to Noelle.

Are you busy?

I don't even bother opening softly with a *Hey, how are you?* I don't have the energy for that. I just want to get to the point.

I place the phone back on the end table and wait for her response. Minutes tick by and, finally, after about fifteen of them, my phone dings with an incoming message.

No, what's up?

I send her another message.

Can I call?

This time I keep the thread open. I watch as the little typing bubble pops up. She's answering me. But then it disappears. And then it pops up again. That happens three times and minutes pass. I wonder what the hell she's going to say. But when the message comes through, it's just one word.

Yes.

Somehow, the period on the end seems hostile. I sigh and think about avoiding the phone call. I know I need to warn her, but I also know that it's going to go over like a lead balloon.

Instead of avoiding it, though, I touch the button that connects me to Noelle's cell phone. I put it on speaker, and I listen as it rings once, twice, and then she picks up.

"Hey, what's up?" Noelle asks.

I clear my throat.

"Have you seen the news?" I ask.

Noelle goes silent. Not the reaction that I was expecting.

"Yeah," she finally says. "I know what you're going to say, Blair," she goes on.

"What am I going to say?" I ask, sounding annoyed, even to myself.

"I know about the murders," she says.

I don't like the way she says it. Almost like it's not a big deal—nothing to be concerned about. I want to tell her this is definitely something to be concerned about.

"And that's it?" I ask.

It comes out far more aggressively than I mean for it to. Immediately, I regret it.

"You wouldn't understand, Blair," Noelle snaps back at me. "You've never let anyone get close to you. Hell, you even keep *me* at arm's length. You don't know the first thing about supporting people. Your family has never known anything about that."

I'm speechless at her words.

I know that I invited it with my snippy question, but what she says hurts. Deeply.

My voice is quiet when I speak.

"I care about you, Noelle," I say evenly. "I think being involved with Jenna is a huge mistake."

"You can think what you want," Noelle says, and then she hangs up the phone.

I sit there, staring at the lock screen on my phone for about thirty seconds before the phone locks itself and goes dark. I can't believe she just hung up on me.

I'm hurt and shocked. Noelle is my oldest, dearest friend. I suddenly feel lost. The idea that I could really lose her over this occurs to me.

And that's even scarier than going out to the lake tonight.

I TRY my best to take a nap in the afternoon, but to no avail. My conversation with Noelle keeps running around in my head, haunting me more than I want it to. The more I think about it, the angrier I get at her. She's being reckless, disregarding what's going on. I get it, I really do. Sometimes people hold a sway over us that we can't explain. I feel like my father's memory does that to me. So maybe I don't understand entirely, but I understand on *some* level.

I also understand the desire to rewrite history.

That I understand on a deep level.

These thoughts are with me all afternoon, circulating on repeat in my head. The conversation plays over and over again, like a highlight reel of bad plays during a football game. It's painful to watch, but I don't seem to have any control over it.

Finally, I get up and make myself some coffee. It's

been a long day, and I know the night ahead is probably going to be just as long, if not longer. Cash has a propensity for long nights. Sometimes I think he might be a vampire himself.

I cup the coffee mug in my hands, letting the warmth radiate into my palms, grounding me in the present and giving me a slight reprieve from my thoughts of Noelle. For a brief instant, I'm alone in my house, here in the here and now. It doesn't last long, but I treasure it while it does. For a second, I feel peaceful. I'm not thinking about the night ahead or the morning that just passed.

I drink the coffee slowly and as I finish off the mug, my phone dings.

I run to it, hoping that it's Noelle. I hope it's her telling me she's sorry, opening the door for me to apologize, too. Opening the door for us to make up and her to come to her senses.

But when I get to it, I see Cash's name. The notification is from him. A text.

I swipe it, opening my messaging app.

Pick you up at 9?

I want to tell him that's far too late. And ridiculous. And stupid. The idea of going out to the crime scene after dark isn't appealing to me at all. But then I think about the conversation I just had with Noelle, and I feel like if I'm going to save her from this, I'm going to have to go out there tonight. I'm not sure what we'll see, if anything, but it feels like the police aren't moving quickly enough. They didn't take us seriously when we contacted them.

I have a hard time believing that they took anyone else seriously. Especially anyone with any ties to the vampire community, who are precisely the people that would have the best idea of what's going on.

The whole thing feels a little bleak.

Going out there tonight is the least I can do. And who knows? Maybe we'll find something they missed.

Sounds good.

I shoot back the text after a moment or two. I don't have much choice.

I take a shower and get ready, finding one of my heaviest sweaters to wear, knowing that we're going to be exposed to the elements out at the lake. And at the end of October, at night, Oklahoma is cold. I grab a scarf and some gloves just in case it's colder than I imagine it will be.

By 8:45, I'm standing at the window, waiting for Cash to pull up.

And right at 9:00, his headlights turn down my long drive and he parks in the circle driveway. I grab my purse and head out the door, locking it behind me. I jog down the steps and the cold air nips at my exposed skin. Maybe the scarf and gloves weren't a silly idea. I imagine it's even colder out at the lake, exposed to the wind on the shore.

I climb up into the cab. Cash is also wearing a sweater, and I notice immediately how handsome he looks in it. He looks like a guy that you'd bring home to meet your parents. A guy on his way to Thanksgiving with his new girlfriend. The thought makes me blush. I don't have parents to bring him home to, though. And possibly not even a best friend, either.

That thought brings any romantic notions crashing down.

"You okay?" he asks, his eyes searching my face. It must be apparent how I'm feeling.

"Fine," I tell him, forcing a bright smile.

Cash doesn't return it. He just stares at me, reading me.

"You're full of shit," he says. "You called Noelle, and it didn't go well, did it?"

"Jesus. You could take this show on the road," I tell him, closing the door and buckling my seatbelt.

"It took awhile, but I feel like I'm getting the hang of reading you," he says, pulling out of the drive.

His statement makes me blush in the darkness. I think about the other night at Noelle's housewarming party. The way he acted toward me. Then I think about us, curled up together on the couch, falling asleep against each other.

But then he left in the middle of the night.

And nothing has really happened between the two of us.

Maybe I'm convincing myself of something that's not really there.

"You look really nice tonight," Cash says in the darkness as he drives.

It catches me off guard, right after my most recent thought.

"You do, too," I reply. "You look like you're going to meet your girlfriend's parents, not investigate the site where two bodies were dumped," I tell him.

He smirks. I smile over at him and he looks at me. It's just a little too long that his eyes linger on me.

"Hey, watch the road," I tell him, clearing my throat and suddenly feeling very exposed.

I think about what he just said about getting better at reading me. I wonder if he can tell what I'm thinking right now. Jesus, I hope not.

Hell, I hope most of the time he's not aware of what I'm thinking. Especially recently.

Unless, of course, he's thinking the same thing.

"I'll look where I want," he says, his voice suddenly husky. My eyes widen. His chiseled jaw is shadowed in the green light of the dash. I feel my heart beat faster, having everything to do with the way he's looking at me and nothing to do with the dangerous evening unfurling before us. I inhale sharply, after holding my breath, and Cash breaks his gaze.

And it's just in time for him to swerve back into our lane as an oncoming car honks at him.

He chuckles nervously and I do the same. Neither of us say anything else about the moment we just shared. We ride in silence out to the lake, and I can't tell if it's worse this way or if we were trying to make small talk. Finally, he turns off on the road that leads out to the lake.

"Do you know which entrance it is?" I ask.

"I do," he says. "My source gave me some directions."

I nod in the darkness, unsure if he catches it. It's only a few moments before we emerge into a clearing. A parking lot beside the lake. There's a dock. And then I notice taillights. They're slightly obscured by a bush, but they're there. I inhale sharply, almost a gasp.

"Do you see that?" I ask Cash.

"I do," he says. His tone is ominous, like he didn't count on something like this happening once we got out here. I want to point out that this is the number one reason I didn't want to go out here tonight. I resist the urge, though.

"Should we leave?" I ask. My question comes out a little more high-pitched than I mean for it to. I clear my throat, hoping that will get rid of any trace of fear in my voice. But I'm not counting on it.

"Hang on," Cash says.

He kills the lights on the truck and creeps forward. He stops a good ways from the car and turns the truck off. We sit there in silence, the red taillights glowing from behind the brush. I'm not sure how good of an idea this is.

"What are we doing?" I ask, my voice coming out as a hushed whisper, like I'm afraid that whoever's in that car will be able to hear me. Everything is silent and it's almost deafening inside the truck. Even though I whisper, it seems like it comes out far too loudly.

"Let's watch for a minute," Cash says.

Unable to keep my fear to myself any longer, I speak up.

"Is this a good idea, Cash?" I ask.

He says nothing. Probably because he *knows* it's not a good idea. He doesn't want to argue with me. I turn my attention back to the taillights and then something happens that sends blood coursing faster through my veins.

A figure walks around to the trunk, another figure follows. The two of them open the trunk.

I feel like I'm going to be sick. I have a sinking feeling that I know what's about to happen.

The two of them wrestle with something in the trunk and I gasp when I realize what it is.

It's a body.

They walk over to the other side of the car with it and toss it onto the ground next to the lake. Then the two of them get back into the car and the car pulls away, apparently following another road that leads out of the area. They don't spot us.

"Did they just—"

"Yes," Cash says, cutting me off. His voice is tense.

"What should we do?" I ask.

"You wait here," he says as he unbuckles his seatbelt.

Before I can think of anything intelligent to say to try and sway him in favor of getting the fuck out of here, he's out the door.

"Cash!" I shout, but he doesn't turn around. "Fuck."

I unbuckle my seatbelt and get out of the truck, slamming the door behind me. I march across the dirt and gravel, mentally cursing Cash for this and bracing myself for what I'm going to see.

CHAPTER EIGHTEEN

"BLAIR, COME HERE!" Cash turns and hollers far too loudly, assuming I'm still in the truck. "Oh, there you are." He quiets and points at the ground in front of himself. I walk up slowly, still not entirely sure that I want to see whatever's waiting for me. I grimace as I come around the side of the bushes and find Cash standing over the body.

"Don't you think we need to call 911?" I ask, reaching for my phone in my back pocket.

"Yeah, probably so," he glances at me, and I nod, dialing the number and putting my phone to my ear. I step away from the body as it rings.

"911 Dispatch, what's your emergency?" a woman's calming voice speaks to me through the phone.

"Yes, hi. I think I need to report a dead body," I say,

sounding unsure of myself. "I mean, I *do* need to report finding a dead body."

"Where are you?"

"Lake Draper," I say. And then I give her the directions to the entrance we took.

"Police are on their way right now," the woman says.

"Thank you," I tell her. And then, after assuring her that I don't need to stay on the phone, I hang up.

"Uhh, Blair," Cash says to me. I look over at him and he's staring down at the body, the flashlight on his phone lighting it up. I really don't want to walk over there and get a good look at it. I cringe inwardly.

"What?" I call, keeping my distance.

"Just come look and tell me something," Cash says.

"Fuck," I mutter under my breath.

I head over to where Cash is going as slowly as I can. I'm dreading whatever he's got over there waiting for me. All I can imagine is another dead body, another of Jenna's friends. And my stomach flips when the thought occurs to me that this time, it could be Noelle.

I pick up my pace then as my hands and face grow clammy. Suddenly my sweater is too hot. I want to strip out of it, feel the cool night air on my skin.

I step up silently next to Cash and look down at what his flashlight shines at.

And when I see it, shock washes over me. Not because it's my best friend, but because what I'm looking at is grotesque and it takes me a moment to process it.

Lying on the ground is a mannequin, dressed in gothic clothing, made up with smokey eye makeup and red lipstick. There are two painted marks on the mannequin's neck. Vampire bites. And it's clear who it's supposed to be.

"Jenna," I whisper.

"Right?" Cash asks. "That's what I saw, too. I wanted you to confirm it."

"Well, it certainly looks like her."

My heart pounds. I was fully expecting to see Noelle, dead on the bank of the lake. I swallow, but my mouth is dry, making it difficult.

"Are you alright?" Cash asks.

"I'm fine," I say a little too quickly.

Cash is silent for a moment, but he stares at me, like he's reading an open book.

"Really, I'm fine," I reiterate.

"You thought it was Noelle," Cash says quietly.

I feel myself begin to get emotional. Tears threaten to spill over onto my face and my throat clenches, making it difficult to speak. I cough.

"Yeah," I admit.

Cash steps closer to me and puts an arm around me. He squeezes me tight to him, turning me into him until I'm face to face with his chest. He wraps his arms around me, and I do the same, relaxing into his embrace. A sob chokes its way out of my throat.

"Hey," Cash whispers. "It's okay. Noelle is safe."

"But for how long?" I ask, pulling away from him. I sound like a little girl, scared of the monster under her bed. Cash looks down at me and places his hands on my upper arms, squeezing them.

"Listen to me, Blair," he says. "We are going to figure this out before it comes to that."

I look up at him, doubtful. I know that Cash will do everything in his power to make that true, but I don't know if we're going to be able to do it quickly enough. I swipe at the tears that have managed to streak down my cheeks.

"I promise you that," Cash says.

"Don't promise," I tell him, placing a hand on his chest.

"Blair, when I promise something, I mean it," he says.

I think about all the people in my life that have promised me things and then never saw them through. All the promises from my dad. Like telling us he would be home for Christmas. Birthdays. Graduation.

He taught me never to believe anyone's word.

It's hard to even wrap my mind around the idea that Cash means what he's saying. But I look back at all that he's done for me. He's never broken a promise. Then again, he's never had to promise me anything quite this serious.

I still feel uneasy, even though part of me wants

desperately to trust him and lean into that feeling of security.

The past tells me not to do that. Nothing is a sure thing.

"Thank you," I tell him. I don't know what else to say. I don't want to tell him that I have my doubts. I'm sure that would hurt him and that's the last thing I want. I'm already hurting too much. Causing him any pain would just make that worse, and besides, I don't want that for him either.

He hugs me tightly. I inhale the scent of his cologne, something woody and masculine. All I smell now is the comfort of his presence.

"You don't have to thank me," Cash says. His voice is low, almost husky.

It would be comical, the two of us hugging each other over a mannequin made up like Jenna, if it weren't for the fact that all I can think about is that Noelle might be next.

"There's no telling who did this," Cash says, thinking aloud. "It could be someone who admires the killer, or it could be the killer himself, sending a warning. Or Jenna trying to throw the scent off herself."

I shudder at the thought. We were so close to them. And there were two of them. Could it be two people acting together?

"Cash," I say slowly. "There were two people out here tonight, weren't there?"

"Yes," Cash confirms simply.

A dangerous thought rolls through my mind like a black storm cloud. Those two people could have been Jenna and Peter. Maybe trying to throw the authorities off her scent. Make it look like someone wanted *her* dead, too. The mannequin was meant to be a threat to her life, maybe?

Could Noelle know what's going on? Be an accomplice?

Could that have been Jenna and *Noelle* out here tonight?

Jesus Christ.

The fact that I can even fathom this scares me.

But Noelle did go along with her in the past. I wonder if the police have even questioned Jenna yet.

Surely, with the news story that broke the other day. They know there's a connection between the victims. And that connection is Jenna. Who's spending all her time with Jenna right now? Noelle.

There's no way that Noelle is unaware if this is what's going on.

I turn around and promptly vomit on the ground.

"Hey! Blair, are you okay?" Cash asks.

I vomit again, though this time nothing comes up. Two more dry heaves follow.

Before I can even swipe at my mouth, Cash is beside me, a comforting hand rubbing circles on my back.

"I'm okay," I tell him, even though I'm not sure that's the case at all.

I look up at him.

Concern is etched on his features. He furrows his brow, and his mouth is a firm line, telling me quite plainly that he doesn't believe me.

"I just had a really disturbing thought," I tell him. "What if Jenna is behind all of this?"

"That's a possibility," he says, but his tone tells me he's a little confused as to why that would be disturbing.

"And Noelle is with her constantly right now. And she went along with a murder plot Jenna hatched all those years ago. What if it was them that we saw?" I ask.

The confusion leaves his face, replaced by real concern. Cash seems to roll this over in his mind, weighing it and measuring it. It alarms me that he doesn't immediately tell me it's a crazy idea. Suddenly, I feel like I could throw up again.

"I see what makes you think that," he says calmly. "But you've known Noelle a long time. And if Jenna was involved, I imagine the police would have arrested her after the second murder. I'm guessing she had an airtight alibi."

"What? That Noelle was with her?" I counter.

"No, it would have to be better than that," Cash assures me.

I sigh deeply.

The two of us stand there over the mannequin, waiting for the cops to show up.

. . .

AFTER ANOTHER MINUTE or two passes, the sound of a siren wails in the distance, growing closer every second. Finally, I see lights turning in at the entrance we used. A police SUV shines a spotlight on the area, and Cash and I shield our eyes with our hands. I squint.

The vehicle pulls up right in front of us, lights shining brightly over the mannequin.

The cop gets out and slams his door.

"I understand you folks found a dead body," he says, walking toward us with a handheld flashlight shining. It's impossible to see his face.

"That's what we thought originally," Cash says, and then he points down at the ground in front of him.

The cop lowers his flashlight and looks the mannequin over.

I look at his face and see him raise his eyebrows.

"A mannequin?" he asks.

"That's what it looks like," Cash says. "But I think it might be a little more significant than being just a mannequin."

"Why's that?" the cops asks, skepticism and annoyance in his voice. I imagine they get people playing armchair detective all the time.

"Well, it's made up just like that gal who got out of prison recently. You know, the one on the news years ago for attempted murder. That vampire group. And then there was another news story saying that two of her old friends have died since she got out of prison. Take a good look at it," Cash says.

The cop steps forward and squats, getting close to the mannequin.

"Was it just one person that dumped it?" he asks.

"Two," Cash says.

"Male or female?"

"It was way too dark to tell," Cash says.

The cop stands up and looks around the area, shining his light on Cash's truck.

"What were you two doing out here?" he asks, suddenly turning his suspicion on us.

I look to Cash and open my mouth to speak but Cash does so first.

"Fishing," he says.

"Fishing, huh?" the cop asks with a chuckle. Then he gives me a lascivious look that I don't appreciate at all. I wrap my arms tightly over my chest, feeling like he's undressing me with his eyes.

"Yeah," Cash says. And he picks up on the vibe, too. He steps forward, in front of me. I'm grateful for that. "We just wanted to let you know what happened," he adds.

"Well, I'll need a statement from the two of you, and we'll get people out here to check it out. Might be a lead on those murders. Might be a prank," he says.

"We'll be happy to help," Cash says.

CHAPTER NINETEEN

BY THE TIME we get back to the house, I'm completely exhausted. I unbuckle my seatbelt and look at the clock. It's only midnight. Technically, an early night for me and Cash. Usually on these adventures we're up well past the witching hour. But this time it's different. I have a good reason for being totally worn out. I genuinely thought that the mannequin was a dead body.

And that the dead body was Noelle's.

I sigh before getting out of the truck.

"Do you want me to come in for a while?" Cash asks.

I know it's his way of checking on me. Lending support and comfort. I feel guilty to take him up on it, though. I know my intentions aren't entirely pure. Self-ishly, I just want to be with him more. I'll be fine on my own. But there's a part of me that wants him in the house with me, on my couch, snuggled up against me.

"I'll be fine," I tell him.

"You sure?" he asks, like he doesn't believe me at all.

In that moment, I'm almost positive he's going to act like he knows better and follow me inside. I smile.

"I'm fine. Really," I say. "Besides, all I'm going to do when I get in there is go to bed."

Cash clears his throat and looks away and I wonder for just a second what's on his mind. He looks back at the dash.

"If you promise you're alright," he says. "I'll leave you in peace." He turns back to me and smirks.

"I solemnly swear that I'm absolutely fine, Mr. Kelly," I say, smirking now, too.

"Then get out of my truck," he says teasingly.

Without another word, I slip out and offer him a wave goodbye before I shut the door. I head up to the porch and grab my keys, unlocking the door. It isn't until I shut the door behind myself that he heads out of the drive. There's something sweet about it. The fact that he wants to make sure I get into the house safely.

I watch through the window as his taillights head for the road and turn out, disappearing into the night. There's a part of me that wishes I had taken him up on his offer to stay. Suddenly, the house feels too big and lonesome. It dawns on me how much more like home it feels when Cash is here with me.

It's probably just because he helped me make it a home by figuring out the haunting that I had going on when I first bought the house. That's all it is. Right?

It's just nostalgia for those weeks we spent here together. I'd been alone for so long—my dad missing and my brother avoiding me except when he needs money—that having someone in the house with me felt nice. Cozy. Like I had a family again.

And with Noelle involved with Hooper since that time, I haven't seen that much of her. And even less now that Jenna's out of prison.

I sigh.

I turn to face the long hallway that leads to the living room. I look at the staircase that leads upstairs to my bedroom. I head for the living room, making a compromise in my mind. I'm really not ready to go to bed, but I also don't want to stay up all night. So, I settle for grabbing my laptop and taking it to bed.

I head upstairs with the laptop in tow and switch on my bedside lamp. I place the laptop on the comforter and go to my closet to change into pajamas. I switch on the television and crawl under the covers, situating my laptop on top of my legs and crack it open.

I open the web browser and then grab my remote. As the browser loads, I find a show to put on in the background. I find myself drawn to one of the channels that primarily specializes in spooky content. Maybe it's Cash's influence. Maybe it's so I can feel closer to my dad. I'm not sure. I never had any interest in any of this stuff until I experienced it first-hand. And I'm still not ready to fully embrace the idea that Cash and I didn't suffer from a shared delusion.

I look back at my laptop and type a few words into the search engine.

real vampire message board

The first result is a subreddit. There's another result for a roleplaying group on Facebook. Finally, near the bottom of the first page of results is the site I'm actually after. The one where I found the first post that seemed to relate to the first murder.

I navigate to the board where I saw that first message.

I scan through the most recent posts and see nothing about someone dumping a mannequin or hinting at anything like that. But then I see a post that catches my attention, just like the first one did.

Another victim

That's the title.

I click on it.

I'm back with an update for you guys. I took my second life tonight. This time a male victim. His blood was different than the female's. Harsher, tangier. Not quite as sweet. I wonder if it had to do with the drugs that were in his system. He also got to enjoy a final sunset at the lake.

Until next time,

Mr. D

My heart thunders in my chest, deafening me as the blood rushes past my ear drums.

Holy shit.

Ho-ly shi-it.

It's the same guy.

I'm certain of it. And I have a distinct gut feeling that this guy isn't someone claiming credit for these murders but not actually committing them. This guy is the real deal. He's the perpetrator that's terrorizing Oklahoma City. Or at least a small group of people in OKC, by the looks of the last two crimes.

I reach for my phone. My first instinct isn't to call the police, but instead to call Cash and hopefully catch him before he makes it all the way home.

The phone rings once before he picks it up, and I hear the sounds of a truck engine in the background.

That's good.

"Hey," he says. "Everything okay?"

"Everything's fine, yeah," I say. "But I found something you might want to see."

"What is it?"

"Another post. On that forum. The vampire one."

"Oh, my God," he says. "About the mannequin?" he asks.

"No," I say. "Nothing about the mannequin. Better than that. It's about the second murder."

I hear the sound of tires squealing as he slams on the breaks. I wonder what street he's on.

"Making a u-turn right now," he says. "Be there in 10."

CASH IS BACK at the house within minutes. I open the door, and he storms in.

"Where's your computer?" he asks.

"It's uh—" I hadn't taken it out of the bedroom. "Upstairs," I say.

Without stopping to worry about it, he takes the stairs two at a time. I have to jog to keep up with him. He turns into my bedroom, and I follow him. I slide onto the bed and pat the other side, telling him to take a seat next to me.

He takes a seat on top of the comforter, and I pull the laptop up until it's touching my crossed legs.

"Here," I say, and I turn it toward him.

He starts to read. I watch his face for a reaction.

His brow furrows and his mouth goes into a grim frown. This is serious.

"Should we call the cops?" I ask.

"Twice in one night?" he counters.

I nod, seeing his point.

"And they didn't take it seriously the last time we told them about one of these posts," he says.

"That's true," I say.

It seems bad not to tell them about it, though.

"What can we do?" I ask.

"I think I know who we might be able to ask for help," Cash says.

CHAPTER TWENTY

"HERE'S HIS E-MAIL ADDRESS," Cash says, showing me a contact card on his phone. "It's my long-time friend, Jonah. We've known each other since college. He works for the newspaper, and he'll probably be more help to us than the police."

I type his e-mail address into the recipient field on the e-mail I'm drafting. And then I go to work on it.

Hi, Jonah.

My name is Blair Graves, and I work for your friend, Cash Kelly. We wanted to see if you could tell us any updated information about the vampire killings in Oklahoma City. Also, we can point you in the direction of a new lead.

Thank you for your time,

Blair Graves

"How does that look?" I ask Cash.

He takes a minute to read over the e-mail and then nods his head.

I hit send.

"Can I look at that again?" Cash asks, pointing at my laptop.

"Sure," I pass it back over to him. He navigates back to the web browser. He does some clicking around and then furrows his brow some more.

"I really don't think this is Jenna," he tells me.

I breathe a sigh of relief. The thought that it's not Jenna is hugely comforting. Because that means that Noelle isn't involved. Right?

"Who do you think it is?" I ask.

"Well, it could be any of the people that ran around in that group. Or it could be someone upset that they tarnished the vampire reputation, such as it were," he says.

"Like some vigilante vampire wanting to set the record straight?" I ask. "Hardly seems like a good PR move to kill some people who made you look bad."

"You're right about that," Cash says. "Then again, we're dealing with someone who literally believes they are a vampire," he says. "Or maybe they really are," he adds under his breath.

"You don't seriously believe that's a possibility, do you?" I ask with a nervous laugh.

"Stranger things have happened," he says.

"Stranger than vampires being *real*?" I ask, my voice going up in pitch at the end of the sentence.

"Stranger than vampires being real," Cash confirms.

I hesitate to ask what that might be, afraid that whatever Cash says, it'll be too hard to believe.

"How can you still struggle with that after all that you've experienced?" he asks me, closing the laptop and turning to face me on my bed.

"Philosophical questions are best left for after midnight," I say with a chuckle, almost to myself. "I don't know, Cash. I still have a hard time believing that any of the things we experienced were real. Couldn't there be other explanations?"

"I'm really interested to hear what you think another explanation for any of it might be," he says.

"Well, the Bigfoot could have been some animal. Maybe wounded, sounding different than it did previously. Maybe it was one of the people that had been at the festival trying to prank Katie," I add.

Cash rolls his eyes.

"And Hattie Solomon?" he asks. "And Duke? Who you saw with your own eyes?"

I stand up from the bed.

"I don't know what to tell you," I say, crossing my arms and beginning to pace at the foot of the bed, feeling a little like a cornered animal being made to share my most intense personal beliefs. Beliefs that make me feel entirely too vulnerable.

"I think there's a reason that you don't want to believe," Cash says.

"So, what if you're right?" I ask, the question coming out more aggressively than I mean for it to.

"What is it, Blair?" he asks. "You can tell me."

I feel the sting of tears in my eyes. I wasn't expecting to get emotional over this, but when I think about it, it's highly emotional. I tell myself there's no reason to be ashamed of that, but vulnerability has never been my strong suit. Not since my dad taught me that it was a weakness over all those years he spent emotionally distancing himself from me and Blake.

"I just—" I begin, trying to verbalize what I'm feeling.

I feel naked, trying to say this to Cash. I don't like it. It's too much.

"What is it?" he coaxes softly.

I can't deny that Cash makes me feel safe. But there's a part of me that knows there's a danger in that. A danger that I could really and truly fall for him and get hurt in a way that I've never been hurt before. Except once. By another man that abandoned me when I needed him.

"If I accept all of this," I say, pausing. "That will mean that I have to consider the possibility of what actually might have happened to my dad."

Cash is silent for a moment, almost like he hadn't expected that to be my answer.

"Blair," he says. "I'm so sorry. I hadn't thought about it that way."

"I didn't expect anyone to," I say, shrugging my shoulders. "But if ghosts are real and Bigfoot is real and vampires are real, what really happened to him? And how long did I spend hating him thinking that he was taking advantage of people when really, he was just looking for the truth, Cash?"

I can hear the desperation in my voice.

I clear my throat and go on.

"That's why it's hard for me to accept any of this. It's easier just to pretend that I've been living in a fantasy world for the last year."

Cash looks at me. There's so much compassion in his eyes that it physically pains me. He stands up and walks over to where I'm standing.

"Come here," he says, wrapping his arms around me.

I let him, and I sink into his embrace, not wanting it to come to an end. I want to stay here, just like this, as long as we can. I feel myself on the verge of tears. I choke them back.

"Cry if you need to, Blair," he says.

And that's all it takes. The floodgates open and I'm soaking his sweater with salty tears. I heave a sob and cry some more. He holds me up and I start to feel lightheaded.

"Here," he leads me back over to the bed. He pulls back the covers and then picks me up, one arm under my knees and another behind my back. Like I'm nothing. I feel weightless in his arms. He lays me down in the center of the bed and then crawls in beside me, fully clothed. He puts his arm out for me to lay my head on, and I relax against him.

I'm struck by the same feeling—that I want to stay like this as long as we can. I know he'll have to leave. And I also know I don't have the courage to tell him how I really feel. In a way, it's pointless. I don't know that I'll *ever* be able to tell him how I really feel.

He pulls me close and grabs my hand, holding it snugly.

"Go to sleep," he says. "I'll be here."

I lean further into him. I hear the beat of his heart through his sweater. And I could swear that it's pounding. Maybe it's wishful thinking, or my own heartbeat in my ear tricking me. I could swear to it, though.

I tuck my hand, holding his, up under my chin and I still myself. I relax. I feel safe.

And then I drift off to sleep.

CHAPTER TWENTY-ONE

IN THE MORNING, I wake and I reach for Cash. But he's gone.

I'm hit with a sinking feeling. The feeling of abandonment. I know it all too well. I feel empty and at a loss. Like the wind was sucked out of my sails when they had been flying high. I wanted nothing more than to wake up to him next to me, still holding me.

I throw my feet out of bed and stand up, stretching.

It's a little after sunrise. Bright light shines in through the sheer curtains that line my balcony. I reach for my phone on the nightstand and check it for a message from him. Maybe something explaining why he had to leave, but there's nothing.

No word.

I feel sick suddenly. I'm mad at myself that I allowed thoughts of what might be to infect my heart. Even if it was only for a night. It was enough.

I place the phone back down and head downstairs.

As I'm padding down the stairway, I hear something. I pause. The sound of sizzling. Like something might be on fire. I pick up my pace and whip around toward the kitchen when I reach the ground floor. I jog over to the doorway and I'm shocked when I see that the sizzling sound was because someone is cooking breakfast.

Cash stands at my stove and monitors a pancake in the skillet.

"I thought you left," I say, and it comes out far more emotional than I mean for it too. My voice is almost breathy. I tell myself it's because I just jogged down the stairs and the hall, but I know that's not the real reason why.

He turns with a wide grin.

"No. I just wanted to do something nice for you," he says.

"Thank you," I say as I look over the spread. There's fruit on the table in the dining room. He's busy stacking up the pancakes, and it looks like one plate is already done. Syrup and butter sit next to the dish of strawberries and blueberries. "I wouldn't have taken you for the domestic type."

"I'm full of all kinds of surprises, Blair," he says with a smirk on his face.

I blush and feel it all the way down to my collarbone. I look away.

Cash turns back to the stove. I clear my throat.

"Is there anything I can do to help?" I ask.

"Just have a seat. You had a rough night," Cash says.

"I don't want you to feel like you need to take care of me," I say, sounding somewhat defensive. Why can't I just let him do something nice for me? I think it's tied up in all the things I was thinking last night about vulnerability and the men in my life. "I'll be fine," I add, sounding even *more* defensive despite my best effort to keep it from coming out that way.

Cash turns around and looks at me.

He points at me with the spatula.

"You know it's okay to need people, right?" he asks.

I'm taken aback by the question. I wasn't expecting that. I don't know how to answer.

"Of course," I say abruptly, biting down on my actual internal response, which is that it's absolutely not okay to depend on any other person at any time. You need to be okay on your own because you will always be on your own. We're born alone and we die alone.

I don't say anything else.

He still stands there, pointing at me with the spatula, a skeptical look on his face. Like he doesn't quite believe the words I'm saying.

"Shouldn't you be focused on the pancakes?" I counter, giving him a look that I hope tells him there's no room for more conversation on the subject. At least not this early in the morning.

"I'm a good multi-tasker," Cash says.

"No one's a good multi-tasker," I retort. "There have been studies that have shown that over and over again. I think you need to focus on the pancakes." I can't help myself, as I say it, I smirk.

"Fine," he says, but he's smirking, too. And the way he says it makes me think that he's not done with this conversation. We'll be revisiting it later. The thought is at once anxiety-inducing and comforting. The fact that he cares is something. I just don't want him to disappear.

I think ever since that happened with my dad, I've been fearing that it'll happen again to someone I care about. Even thinking that Noelle might be killed brought it to the surface.

Cash turns back to the stove and continues on with his cooking. I go to the fridge and grab the bottle of orange juice and pour myself a glass. I ask him if he wants some and he nods. I pour him a glass, too. I place it next to the stove. I stand next to him and lean against the counter.

"Are you monitoring my progress?" Cash asks, not looking away from the food. "It's fine if you are. I work well under pressure."

"I wasn't," I say. Instead, I am lost in my own thoughts, wondering how to patch things up with Noelle. "I was thinking about Noelle."

"And wondering exactly how you're going to have a conversation with her in which she doesn't get mad at you for asking very relevant questions?" Cash asks, still not looking away from the pancakes. He places another one on a plate.

"Basically, yes," I say.

"I don't know exactly what you need to say, but I think you do need to try to talk to her again," Cash says.

"Are you sure?" I ask. "She wasn't really happy with what I had to say the last time."

Cash looks up at me now.

"Blair, she's your best friend, isn't she?" he asks.

"She is," I say.

"You don't want that relationship to end," he says. And the way he looks at me when he says it makes me think he really gets it. The fact that I don't have that many more people left in my life that I can count on. It makes me unexpectedly emotional, and I walk over to the table and take a seat. Mostly so he won't see my face right now and perceive anything more than I want him to.

But he turns around and looks at me after he pours the batter for another pancake.

"I know what it's like to feel alone," Cash says. "And when you have those relationships that are truly meaningful to you, you need to hold on to them. As tightly as you can," he adds. He stands there, looking at me for a moment. I look up at him.

He's right. I know he is. I also know that it's going to be incredibly awkward to have this conversation with Noelle. I'm dreading it. I'm not good at vulnerability and apologizing includes *a lot* of vulnerability. I'm in my thirties; this should be easier. But I blame my dad for that. Maybe he could have done a better job at teaching me that vulnerability was alright.

But he didn't.

And here we are. Me, in my thirties, having to grow up all over again.

"You're right," I say to him. "I know you are."

"I know it's hard," Cash says. "I'm about as good as you are at opening up to people," he adds with a sad chuckle.

"You are," I tell him. But I smirk now.

It's something about our relationship that just works. That both of us are hesitant to really let anyone in. It's allowed us to move slowly with our friendship, revealing things only when either of us were ready to. It works for us.

And for that, I'm grateful.

"I'll call her later," I tell him. "All I want to think about right now is those pancakes," I add with a genuine smile. I'm touched that he stayed and bothered to make breakfast for the two of us.

Cash smiles and turns back to the stove. I sit there, watching him as he finishes breakfast and I feel incredibly grateful for the relationship that we do have, no matter what it turns into.

. . .

IT'S LATER in the day when I find myself alone in the house, my phone sitting in front of me, and the only task remaining for the day to call Noelle and apologize. Try to smooth things over. Even if I don't necessarily feel sorry for telling her the truth, I need to keep the line of communication open between us. That's essential if anything is going to threaten her safety. I know that much. And that makes me willing.

I pick up the phone and tap her contact card. I'm about to dial her when a text message pops up on the screen.

It's from Noelle.

> Hey.

That's all it says.

Somehow, the one word message fills me with dread. What's going to come next?

Is she still angry?

Jesus, I hate confrontation. Especially with people I love. It's not so bad with people I don't care that much about. But with my best friend? This is a nightmare. All I can think is that I'm going to lose her for good.

> Hey, I was just about to call you.

I see the little bubble pop up, letting me know she's typing. As soon as it disappears, a message comes through.

Really? Why?

I'm still unable to get a solid read on how she's feeling. I feel my heart beat faster.

I type out a message, deciding to just be up front and honest.

> I just wanted to apologize to you for upsetting you the other day. I love you and I'm just worried about you with everything that's going on.

This time, a bubble doesn't pop up right away. It's a minute before that happens and it seems to stretch on infinitely.

Finally, it does, and she sends another message shortly thereafter.

I understand, Blair. It is getting a little spooky.

My eyebrows shoot up. Could this be Noelle realizing what danger she might be in?

What does Hooper say about all of it?

In a moment, another message comes through, and Noelle sounds more like Noelle than she has since Jenna got out of prison.

Well, you know he was just as in love with her in high school as most of the guys we went to school with. And she didn't give any of them the time of day back then. Things haven't changed much, so he's just as annoyed about me spending time with her as you are.

I do remember that.

Even after everything happened—after I came into the picture—so many guys were still obsessed with Jenna. It was kind of weird. But maybe not. A lot of kids romanticize criminals. I know there was a period where a girl in our class would bring a serial killer encyclopedia to school every day and talk about how cute Jeffrey Dahmer was.

According to her social media accounts, she seems to have turned out okay.

I don't think that's entirely that uncommon.

As a teenager, everything feels like life and death, and you're trying to taste life at its fullest. Figure out who you are. Play right on the edge.

Does that bother you?

A bubble pops up and then a message.

It's annoying.

I write back.

> That's understandable.

After a few moments with no response, Noelle texts again.

> Anyway, the reason I messaged you wasn't only because I missed you, although I do miss you. I wanted to extend an olive branch and invite you to the party at the high school for the teachers. Tickets are $25 and it benefits the school. It should be fun! Hooper and I will be there!

I hesitate to ask the one question that comes to the forefront of my mind: *will Jenna be there?*

What does it matter? Maybe she will, maybe she won't. It's not like I have any control over that. I just wish Noelle would get away from her. And maybe she will. Jesus, I hope so.

Instead, I just send back this message:

> I'll take two.

CHAPTER TWENTY-TWO

THAT EVENING, I curl up on the couch and put on the TV and try to find something to watch. Once I cycle through all the cable channels and don't find something that sparks my interest, I head over to my favorite streaming service, home of all the *Real Housewives* shows. I pick one at random and start from the beginning of the season. Trash reality TV is a balm to my wounds, and right now I'm still worried over what's going on with Noelle.

This is a nice distraction.

But I don't get to enjoy it for long.

My phone dings. But it's not the sound for a message. It's my e-mail. And there's only one person I'm waiting for an e-mail response from: Jonah.

I grab it and swipe to open the notification before I can even read who it's from. And sure enough, it's the e-mail I was waiting on.

I read it and then read it again, not sure that I'm reading what I think I am. This is a lead that we ruled out, isn't it?

There's only one thing to do, even though it's close to midnight.

I call Cash.

WEARING gray sweatpants and a worn-out t-shirt, Cash shows up on my doorstep, apparently as close to going to sleep as I was before the e-mail came through.

"So, show me this e-mail," he says, standing on my porch in the cold.

"Come inside. Where's your jacket?" I ask.

Cash steps into the house and rubs his hands together. I can see goosebumps on his biceps.

"I didn't bother to grab it. This seemed more important."

"Suit yourself," I say.

I hand him my phone and he reads the e-mail aloud.

"Hi, Blair. I've heard a lot about you. I kind of anticipated that you might reach out over this. I've been doing some digging and kept hitting dead ends. But one person's name kept coming up. Peter Kilmer. I know that in your dad's book, your dad said that this guy didn't want anything else to do with Jenna, but it turns out he was writing to her while she was in prison. We couldn't get any of the letters—an informant at the women's correctional facility told us this—but apparently, they wrote to each other frequently. And it's my suspicion that maybe Peter had something to do with all of this. Maybe a way of getting revenge for everything that Jenna had to go through. I'm not sure. We just found this out tonight and we're going to pass it along to the detectives. But I wanted to keep you in the loop. They also mentioned that he wasn't the only guy writing to Jenna while she was in prison. Thanks, Jonah."

Cash stares at the phone and seems to scan the e-mail again, looking for anything he might have missed.

He hands it back to me.

"Well, shit," he says. "He gave me the same vibe he gave your dad."

"I know. Me, too," I say. "I didn't get the impression that he wanted anything more to do with Jenna."

"Strange that he would be corresponding with her in jail and not see her after she got out," he says.

"Maybe something went wrong," I offer. "Maybe he wanted to get back together with her after she got out and she turned him down. Maybe that was the end of it," I say.

"That could definitely be the case," Cash says.

He seems to be thinking hard about this, trying to come up with something else. Another lead, produced right out of thin air. But he doesn't say anything.

I stand there in silence, too. Thinking about this revelation.

"Well," I say. "If Peter is the killer, and Jonah hands this over to detectives, I guess the whole thing will be over, soon. Won't it?"

I feel a surge of premature relief, thinking that this means that Noelle will be safe. That is, unless Peter gets to her first. I can't imagine that Jenna doesn't have any ill will towards her. Her testimony is what put Jenna away, after all.

"I would guess so," Cash says. "But something about this isn't sitting right with me."

"I agree," I say, the relief leaving as quickly as it came.

Both of us are silent.

Finally, I speak.

"So, what do we do now?" I ask Cash. I want his guidance. I want him to tell me that all of this is going to go away, and my friend will be unharmed.

"I think we just have to wait," he says. "If the cops go talk to him tomorrow and have any reason to, they'll arrest him. And if it's him, all of this will stop."

"You're right," I say.

I know that Cash is right. I know that waiting is the only thing we can do at this point. And it's hell. I want to go down to the station and ask them if they already got the tip from Jonah and what they're going to do about it. I'm not sure that they'd appreciate some random woman walking in there and telling them all how to do their jobs, though.

It might hinder everything more than help it.

Waiting is our only option.

"So, I guess I'll go home. You go to bed, and we'll reconvene in the morning. If we're lucky, there will be a news story first thing about how Peter Kilmer was arrested for the vampire killings in Oklahoma City," Cash offers with a weak smile. I can see in his eyes that he doesn't believe for a second that Peter is responsible. It fills my gut with dread.

"Yeah," I say meekly. "I guess that's all we can do. And all we can hope for."

"I'll talk to you in the morning, Blair," Cash says.

And then he leaves.

CHAPTER TWENTY-THREE

SOMEHOW, against all odds, I manage to fall asleep in the night. I think it's because of how exhausted I've been over this whole thing. My body just gave out and demanded rest. I wake around nine in the morning and the sun is shining brightly. I stretch in bed and for a moment, none of the vampire stuff is on my mind. For a few peaceful seconds, it's just October and I'm waking up, sleepy and ready for coffee.

But then, as if cued by the stretch, my mind snaps back to the reality of the situation, and I know I need to check the news.

I grab my phone and go to all the local news websites. I check Facebook and other various social media. But I find nothing.

The next news broadcast comes on at ten. And by the time I'm done scouring the internet, it's almost that time.

I head downstairs and turn on the TV, hoping against hope to see that Peter was arrested overnight. That the police think they've found their man, and that because of all this, Noelle will be safe. Though there's a part of me that knows she won't be safe until Jenna fucks right on off. Or Noelle makes her.

And that isn't something I'm willing to count on.

It's hard to get out of a relationship like that. It's manipulative, borderline abusive. I know that those kinds of people can hold sway over others. It's sort of how cults work, and I'm not above saying that the little group Jenna ran was a cult.

I'm not sure that Noelle would ever agree on that with me, but she doesn't have to.

I text Cash as I'm sitting on the couch, waiting for the news to start.

About to watch the morning news. You hear anything yet?

It's only about thirty seconds before he responds.

Nothing yet. I'm about to do the same.

I don't say anything back. There's not really anything *to* say. We're both nervous, I know that. We both want this to end without anyone else getting hurt. And we both feel somewhat powerless to make it stop. We're counting on the detectives to do that. And, with any luck, they did overnight.

Finally, the broadcast starts and immediately, a breaking news banner sweeps across the screen.

A cute girl that can't be more than twenty-five stands there stoically in front of a television screen with a picture on it that I don't recognize.

"Overnight, authorities found another body that seems to be related to the vampire-like killings happening in Oklahoma City. The man, Nolan Jennings, had a connection to the two other victims. All of whom were participants in a role-playing game in the late 1990s. Also, all of the victims knew Jenna Prescott, who recently got out of prison for the attempted murder of her stepfather in 1999."

Nolan stares back at me, a wide grin on his face, apparently at a party somewhere. The snapshot is harmless. The kind of thing that anyone might have in a family photo album. His smile is infectious. And all I can imagine is what he must have looked like, dead on the bank of Lake Draper, two holes in his neck, drained of blood.

I'd rather not think about that, but there it is. The image is crisp in my mind as I remember finding the mannequin out there that looked like Jenna.

"Police have also told us that recently, a mannequin was dumped at the lake made up to look like Prescott in complete goth clothing and makeup. The police have not confirmed who they think might be responsible for that."

Probably teenagers, I think. Kids who don't realize how fucked up this actually is. And they probably won't until their brains fully develop around their mid to late twenties. I find myself feeling like an old lady, annoyed by loud children playing on my lawn.

Could Peter have done this?

There's really no reason he couldn't have, I think.

If he really is still enamored with Jenna, he might be trying to right some wrongs of the past. Maybe make up for what he was unwilling to do when they were kids and punishing everyone who got out of that situation unscathed.

I pick up my phone and call Cash.

He answers on the first ring.

"I guess they didn't arrest Peter," he says.

"I would think they'd have led with that if they had, and maybe there wouldn't have been another murder," I confirm.

"Those are my thoughts," he says.

He sighs on the other end of the call.

"What now?" I ask.

"I think you need to have another heart-to-heart with Noelle," he says.

His tone is grim and he's probably thinking what I've been afraid to put words to after the news broadcast: that there are only a couple of people left that Peter—or whoever it is—might want to take out. It's clear that the killer is targeting people associated with Jenna. And my guess is that Noelle's number is coming up soon.

I feel a knot of dread form in my stomach.

"I know," I say. "I think she might be more receptive to it today than she was previously," I tell him.

"Did you guys make up?" he asks.

"We did," I confirm.

"Well, that's good. I hope she *is* more receptive this time, Blair," he pauses and sighs again. "Because I think she really needs to listen to you. Her life may depend on it."

I say nothing but swallow a lump in my throat.

I don't know if Noelle will listen to me.

But I have to try.

I CALL Noelle and she picks up immediately.

"Have you seen the news?" she asks, breathless.

It catches me off guard, the way she answers the phone. This wasn't what I was expecting to be met with. I was expecting defensiveness again.

"I did. That's why I called," I say. "Are you okay?"

"I'm okay," she says, but her voice is small, possibly even afraid. I hate hearing her like this.

"Do you want to come over?" I ask.

"I don't want to be an imposition," she tells me.

"Noelle, you're never an imposition," I retort.

"I'm just kind of freaked out," she says.

"I wouldn't blame you."

"It's just really hitting close to home now. With a third victim. And all of them being people that I used to know. People that ran in the same circle. And that seems to be the pattern here. People that knew Jenna," she says, her voice growing slightly frantic.

"Breathe," I tell her. "Is Hooper there?" I ask.

"He drove out to Noble to see his parents last night and stayed there. So, I've been alone," she tells me.

Alone isn't how she needs to be right now. I know that much. Even if I can't make things better, at least I can make her feel less alone.

"Tell me what's going on in your head," I tell her.

"I'm scared, Blair," she says. "I'm scared that I'm next. And I'm scared for Jenna. What if she's next?"

I hesitate to respond. My fear here isn't for Jenna at all. I feel like these crimes are being committed *for* her if not orchestrated by her. What if this is all some elaborate plan to get revenge on Noelle for turning on her?

Finally, I speak.

"I can understand why you'd feel that way," I say. "It's frightening. Anyone would be terrified in your position," I tell her. "Hell, I'm scared. That's why I've been momming you so much. I apologize, but I don't apologize, you know?"

"I know," Noelle says, and then she sighs.

"This is all going to be okay," I tell her.

"How can you be sure?" she asks, her voice going up at the end of the question, almost hysterically.

I hesitate to respond, because I *can't* be sure. And I don't want to tell her that.

"I am going to do everything I can to make sure you are," I tell her.

Noelle is silent for a moment.

"Thank you, Blair," she says.

"Why don't you come over today?" I ask.

"That's probably a good idea," she says. "I'll grab my things and head over."

"I'll see you in a little bit," I say. "Drive safe."

CHAPTER TWENTY-FOUR

I WASH my face and throw my hair in a bun. I put on a sweater and some sweatpants and make some coffee as I wait for Noelle to show up. Finally, about an hour after our phone call, I hear tires in the drive and go to the front door. I swing it wide just as Noelle steps up onto the porch.

"Come in," I tell her.

But before she can do that, she wraps her arms around me in a huge hug. She squeezes me tightly. I squeeze her back, placing one hand on the back of her head.

"It's going to be okay," I assure her. "And you can stay here if you want to," I tell her.

"Thank you," she says. And then she pulls away.

"Come in," I repeat and step out of the way for her to come all the way inside.

Noelle hangs her coat on the rack and heads for the kitchen.

"I made coffee," I tell her.

"I'd love some," she says. "Maybe with some Bailey's," she adds with a dark chuckle.

"You got it," I tell her, heading behind her for the kitchen. I pour her a cup and add Bailey's, then hand it to her. She sips it gratefully.

"Perfect," she says.

I smile at her and pour myself some of the same.

"What time will Hooper be back?" I ask her.

"Tonight," she says. "He's helping his dad with some stuff this afternoon, but he'll be back later."

"You can tell him to come here, if you want," I tell her. "And then he could follow you home, if that would make you feel better. I'll do it if he won't."

"That's a good idea," she says. "I'd like that. I'll send him a text."

And she does. She types it out and I hear the sound of the message sending. She tucks it back into her pocket and sips her spiked coffee.

"Want to go sit down?" I ask her.

She nods and I lead the way into the living room.

There are still TV trays set up in the living room from my makeshift workspace with Cash. I wonder briefly if I should come up with an excuse for why it looks this way but decide against it. It's probably better to say nothing at all. I doubt Noelle's mind will jump to the conclusion that we've been stalking the vampire murders from our headquarters here. And I think at this point, if I did tell her, it would freak her out even more.

She sits down on one side of the couch and I take the seat on the other side, so I can face her.

"How are you doing?" I ask.

"I'm okay," she says. "All things considered. I didn't really like being alone last night. Hooper assured me I'd be alright, but I didn't like that he left. Not in the middle of this."

"Yeah, that would annoy the shit out of me," I tell her.

"Same," she says. "I was super irritated."

"Understandably so, Noelle," I tell her. "Maybe you should talk to him about it."

"I think I will tonight," she says. Then she grows quiet.

"It's going to be okay," I tell her after a few moments. She stares into her coffee.

"I just—" she seems to collect her thoughts. "I think it was a mistake reconnecting with Jenna," she says. "But I felt forced into it. My family is ridiculous. I wish they hadn't asked me to do any of that shit with the homecoming party," she adds. There's pain in her voice.

"I wish they hadn't, either," I say. "Your aunt is a lunatic or an absolute sadist for putting you in that position."

"I agree," Noelle says. "She is that."

"You should never have had to do that," I say. "You should never have been put in a place where you would have to deal with seeing her again."

"Looking back, that's how I feel about it," Noelle says. "You know how I am: I swallow myself to make other people feel better."

It's true. Noelle is terrible about making herself small for the comfort of others. She's always struggled with standing up for herself. And I've always suspected that her relationship with Jenna was the total root of that.

"It's fucked up," I say. "I'm so sorry this is happening."

"Me, too," she says. She sounds defeated.

"Hey," I say.

She looks up at me.

"This is going to be a memory in just a little while. They're going to figure out who's doing this and put a stop to it," I tell her. I hesitate to add that Cash, myself, and Jonah are working on making that happen. I don't want to stress her out more than she already is.

"Part of me believes you," she says. "And part of me thinks I need to watch my back because I'm up next."

"Noelle," I tell her. "You do need to watch your back. I'm not going to deny that. This is dangerous. And the person that's doing this *is* coming after people connected with Jenna." I pause. "Now," I say. "Do you have any idea who it might be?"

Noelle sighs.

"I have no idea," she says. "It could be anyone. A crazy person that fell in love with Jenna while she was in the news, or even someone that hates all of us. I have no idea, Blair," she says.

I nod.

She doesn't include the most obvious possibility. Or at least the most obvious to me.

Jenna.

I push it a little further.

"What about Peter?" I ask.

She looks up at me again, and her face tells me she doesn't think that's a possibility.

"Peter loved Jenna. And he wanted the best for her," she says. "That's the whole reason he didn't go with us that night, and the whole reason he called the cops on her."

"But do you think he could be trying to prove something to her? Make up for lost time?" I ask.

"I really don't think so. They don't talk to each other, at least that I know of," she says.

Apparently, Jenna hasn't bothered to mention her communication with Peter during the time that she was still in prison.

I wonder if there's a reason for that.

If maybe that reason is because Peter is doing her dirty work now.

"Are you sure?" I press the issue.

"I'm sure, Blair," she says. "Jenna isn't in love with him anymore. I'm not sure she ever really was."

It doesn't do much to instill any confidence in me that Peter couldn't be responsible. Even though he didn't give me, my dad, or Cash the vibe that he was. It's still a possibility. People are capable of hiding all sorts of things about their personality. Just look at Ted Bundy.

We fill the afternoon with talk about other things. I do my best to take Noelle's mind off of everything that's going on. Finally, the conversation turns to the Halloween party at the school.

"You're coming, right?" she asks. There's a hopeful note in her voice, accompanied by something else that I can't identify at first. But then it occurs to me that it's fear. She wants me to be there. She doesn't want to go with just Hooper. I wouldn't feel totally safe, either, with a guy who thought it was okay to go out of town in the middle of all of this.

"Of course," I say.

"Is *he* coming with you?" she asks, arching an eyebrow, her tone turning more relaxed.

Now it's my turn to be nervous. I chuckle. I know where she wants to go with this.

"I haven't told him that he is yet," I tell her with a smirk.

"That's kind of gutsy to think that he'll just go along with it, isn't it?" she asks, surprised at my answer.

"I have a feeling he won't want to miss it," I tell her. I don't tell her the whole of that. I imagine Cash will want to go because there's a possibility that Jenna might show up, which could give him a little bit more information on this whole thing.

Cash likes being right in the middle of things.

"That's good," Noelle says. And she smiles. The way she does it makes me think that she's sensing a romance brewing. I hate to correct her. If this keeps her mind off of things, so be it.

I'll let her have her fantasy.

And maybe live vicariously through it, if I'm honest.

CHAPTER TWENTY-FIVE

FRIDAY, the day of the Halloween party, arrives without any more murders.

I don't feel like we can breathe a sigh of relief just yet though. Someone is still out there, stalking the night, biding their time, and waiting for the right moment. My skin wants to crawl off my body at the possibility of another killing.

Cash and I have scoured the message boards, looking for anything that might point us in the direction of a potential lead. But to no avail. Nothing has popped up. Whoever it is must be planning something big. The thought of it makes me sick at my stomach. And Cash and I haven't really talked about it, though I'm sure we're both thinking it.

It seems better to leave it unspoken, to not put that out into the universe. But I can feel it in my gut. Something's coming.

Late on Friday afternoon, I give up the ghost and stop searching for any posts that might point me in the right direction. Instead, I channel my energy into getting ready. Cash convinced me earlier in the week to get an actual costume. I insisted on going as a bat. Mainly because the costume consisted of a fuzzy pullover, wings, and black leggings. Simple and comfortable. Cash decided he'd go as Satan himself. As I put on the last of my makeup, a little droplet of blood on my lip for authenticity, I wonder if Cash is going to go all out.

As a kid, Halloween wasn't my favorite holiday. Mainly because when Blake and I went trick-or-treating, it was with the nanny. Dad always had a show to put on for the holiday. He worked late on Halloween, doing an extra-long special that kept him away from his family. I always wished he was with us.

But no amount of wishing changed the way that things turned out.

I look at myself in the mirror. I look the part of a woman in her thirties going to a Halloween party. I'm even wearing Converse for extra comfort. I remember the days when Noelle and I would dress up in the sluttiest costumes we could find at Spirit Halloween, back when we were in our early twenties. Now all I can think about is how cold my ass would be in a naughty nurse costume. I'm already thinking the bat pullover isn't going to be enough to keep the frosty air from nipping at my legs.

I check my phone, checking the time, and there are two messages waiting for me.

One from Noelle:

> Can't wait to see you tonight!

One from Cash:

> I'm about to head your way.

I answer Cash first.

> Ready already?

He texts back immediately.

> Doesn't take me all day to look at a horseshoe.

I chuckle to myself at the phrase. My dad used to say that. I answer Noelle, then, telling her I'm equally excited to see her. I don't bother to mention that I hope Jenna won't be there. Somehow, if Jenna comes, it seems like it might be a more dangerous situation. What if whoever it is that's killing people shows up because of that?

It's a stretch. How would they know?

Jenna has laid low on social media since she got out. I can't imagine that she's started posting her whereabouts now, especially with a killer on the loose that seems to have an obsession with her.

That is, unless she's involved in some way.

The thought creeps back in at the edges of my mind. I've been trying to keep it at bay all week. I've tried to keep my feet on the ground and my thoughts positive. But the skeptic in me keeps screaming that I'm overlooking something. There's something that we're not putting together.

And I have this sinking feeling that we might get another piece of information tonight.

Whether we want it or not.

I sigh and look in the mirror one last time, then I grab my clutch purse—black with a leather bat wing on it—and head downstairs to wait for Cash to arrive.

I pace the hallway next to the front window. I keep peeking out, wishing he'd hurry up and get here so I didn't have to be alone with my thoughts.

And just as if I conjured him out of the air, he comes pulling down the drive. I hurry out the front door and lock it behind me. Before he can come to a stop, I'm running up to the truck. I let myself in and take a look at him. He's got the full outfit going on. Red sweater, red pants, black shoes, red cape, and black horns. It's completed with red face paint.

"Speak of the Devil and he shall appear," I remark as I put my seatbelt on.

"You're a cute little bat," he says.

I blush at his words but hope he can't tell. And then we're off.

"Moore High School, right?" Cash asks.

"The very one," I say.

"Crazy that we both went there," he says.

"Not really if we both grew up in Moore," I say with a chuckle.

"I suppose you're right," he says. "But I like to believe in serendipity."

He casts a glance over at me and I furrow my eyebrows, not totally able to read his expression under the dramatic face paint he's got going on.

I focus back on the road as we drive out into the night. Cash takes the highway, and we pass downtown Oklahoma City. As I look out over the park, I see trick-or-treaters and adults dressed up for a night out on the town. It's festive, bright, and happy. As we get closer to Moore, I feel myself getting antsy. I shift in my seat.

"You okay?" Cash asks.

"Just uneasy," I say.

"About what?"

"I just have this weird feeling, you know? Like something's going to happen."

Cash seems to think about that.

"What do you think is going to happen?" he asks, sounding somewhat cautious.

"I don't know," I say. "I just have a feeling."

He doesn't say anything else and we get off the highway. My old stomping grounds. As he drives down

Eastern, I remember all the time that Noelle and I spent driving around this part of town when we were teenagers. Only a few miles to the east is the old Graves house. The one that belongs to a surgeon and his wife now. All so I could sell it and split the profit with my brother, who isn't ever *not* in gambling debt.

Cash pulls into the parking lot of the high school, just outside of the basketball auditorium where the Halloween fundraiser is being held. The lot is full of cars. I try to get a grasp on how many people might be there, but I lose count as Cash pulls down the second row, looking for a parking. Finally, he finds one and we get out of the truck.

Out in the night air, I feel vulnerable in my little bat costume. It occurs to me just how thin these leggings are. And it's *cold* tonight.

I step around to the front of the truck and meet him, taking in his devil costume. I laugh.

"What?" he asks.

"I just—I guess I've never seen you dressed up as a devil, that's all," I say with a smirk.

"Well, it would be weird if you had," he snarks back, but there's a smirk on his face, too. "Come on, let's go."

Together, we walk across the parking lot and find the entrance to the auditorium. He swings the door wide, and I'm greeted by the same trophy case that stood here years ago.

"Wow," I say.

"Not much has changed, huh?" he asks.

"Not much at all," I say.

"Sometimes that's a good thing," Cash says, and it seems like the statement is loaded. Like it isn't about the high school auditorium at all. I blush in the darkness.

There aren't many lights and those that are on have been changed out for purple and orange bulbs. We walk down the hallway and find the staircase that leads down to the bottom floor. We pass several party goers that seem to be heading up for a smoke break. We finally get to the bottom floor landing and it's more of the same, though there are a lot more decorations down here.

I spot skeletons sitting next to candy dishes and streamers that are blood red drape over the entrance to the basketball court. I push through and Cash follows. Out there, the floor is lit by multicolored lights. There's even a disco ball hanging from the high ceiling, casting ribbons of reflections across the room.

There's already a crowd. No one's dancing yet, though, except for a couple on the far side of the floor. I scan the room, seeing people lined up at the makeshift bar and gathered in groups at tables that line the court. I search for Noelle and then remember that I have no idea what her costume is for tonight.

That seems important. Maybe I should have asked her about that.

But just as I feel a wave of anxiety about finding her, I spot her.

She's dressed as an angel, standing next to Hooper, who's dressed tastelessly as a vampire, it seems. Noelle doesn't seem bothered. The two of them seem to be in deep conversation and I look back at Cash and nod, then the two of us make a beeline across the floor for them.

"Hey!" Noelle shouts over a classic Halloween song when she sees me. She immediately reaches out and wraps me in a tight hug. It's the kind of hug I'm used to from her.

I squeeze her tightly, too, eager for the affection from her. Eager for the weird curtain between the two of us to come down once and for all. She holds onto me a little longer than necessary, but I'm not about to tell her to let go. I've missed her, even though she hasn't gone anywhere physically. Finally, she lets me go.

"I'm so glad you guys could come," she says, squeezing my shoulders. Then she reaches out a hand to shake Cash's. "Cash, this is my boyfriend, Hooper," she says. Cash nods at Hooper.

"Hey, man," he says.

"Hey," Hooper says, reaching out to shake Cash's hand, too.

"How are you, Hooper?" I ask.

"Fine," he says. But the look on his face says otherwise. His smile is more of a grimace. I briefly think about asking him about it but think better of it. They were in an intense conversation before we came over here. I wonder if they were fighting. The last thing I want to do is get in the middle of that.

"So, how's the party been so far?" I ask, casting a glance behind me at the dance floor. Two other couples have joined the first, dancing out on the floor.

"Slow, so far," Noelle says, but she smiles somewhat sadly.

I'm struck again by the feeling that something isn't right with her and Hooper. I glance over at him. His attention is fixed elsewhere, like he's lost in thought. The costume was a thoughtless choice with what Noelle's dealing with. That's not like him.

Noelle is his dream girl. I wonder what kind of trouble there might be in paradise. I remember the night he sat down with me and told me he was in love with her at the Solomon House.

It makes a sense of sadness wash over me. Maybe everything good comes to an end. It makes me think about me and Cash and whatever is going on between the two of us. It brings me back to the idea that it would be best not to change the dynamic with him.

What if I lost him entirely?

I don't have many friends. I can't afford to lose any of them.

The thought makes a knot form in my stomach.

"Are you guys gonna get drinks?" Noelle asks, looking between me and Cash.

Cash looks down at me as if he's asking me if that's what I want to do.

I nod my head.

"Sure," I say. "Let's go."

"I'll go with you!" Noelle adds a little too brightly.

Cash catches my eye and his brow furrows. Clearly, he's picking up on the same vibe that I am. I nod at Noelle, and the three of us head over and get in line for the bar.

CASH GETS a beer and I get a vodka tonic with lime. Noelle passes on the opportunity for another drink. I pull her off to the side as Cash is getting his drink.

"Are you okay?" I ask.

"Fine," she says, again, far too brightly. Far too quickly. The way someone says it when they don't mean it at all.

"What's going on, Noelle?" I ask.

She sighs, knowing that I know her better than anyone. It's pointless for either of us to lie to the other.

"Hooper and I got into an argument on the way here. We've been fighting a lot lately, actually," she says.

"Well, that's normal, isn't it?" I ask.

"I suppose," Noelle says.

I'm not buying that, though. This is weighing on her.

"You guys will make up," I tell her.

She looks up at me and gives me a pressed smile, like she appreciates the sentiment but doesn't believe it at all.

"I'm sorry," I say, reaching for her hand.

She squeezes mine.

"It's fine," she says. This time it sounds more genuine. Almost like she's already come to terms with the fact that the relationship could come to an end. It saddens me.

"Do you want to break up with him?" I ask.

"No," she says. "I don't. But things have been hard lately," she adds. "I think the whole Jenna thing has stressed him out, too."

"I can't blame him," I say.

"I know," she says. "Both of you just worry about me."

"And rightly so," I say. "She did almost kill someone, Noelle."

"And her friends are dropping dead left and right," Noelle says.

"That, too," I say.

"I need to go to the bathroom," I say. "You wanna go with me?"

Noelle nods, as if she's glad for the opportunity to slip away from Hooper for a few minutes.

I catch Cash's eye as he walks toward us, and I point to the bathroom. He nods, understanding. And the two of us head out of the auditorium to the bathrooms just down the hallway.

We slip in and I sit down to do my business. After I wash my hands, Noelle is still in the stall. I pull out my phone and a notion strikes me: to check the vampire message board.

And I'm not disappointed when I do.

Hello, an update for all of you that are curious about my journey. It's taken a long time to get here, and I've sacrificed the unworthy on my way here. Tonight, it'll be finished right where it started.

The post is short, to the point, and it sends my heart racing.

Finished right where it started.

Jenna's parents' house?

My mouth goes dry as Noelle opens the door to her stall.

"You alright?" she asks with a nervous chuckle, apparently reading the expression on my face.

"Fine," I say, locking my phone and tucking it into my bat purse. I force a smile at her, but she eyes me suspiciously. "Really," I say. "It's just Blake."

She rolls her eyes.

"When are you gonna cut him off entirely, Blair?" she asks.

I hesitate to answer at first. But then I speak softly.

"He's the only family I have left," I say. It comes out more poignant than I mean for it to. And it hits me like a ton of bricks. It's the damn truth. Blake *is* the only family I have left, and now I'm emotional about it when the fucker didn't even text me.

Maybe that's *why* it hits so hard.

I try to shake it off, and we head back out into the auditorium to face the rest of the night.

CHAPTER TWENTY-SIX

NOELLE and I find our way back over to where Cash and Hooper are standing. Cash is talking to Hooper when we get back over there. Well, talking *at* him is probably more accurate. Hooper sort of looks like a deer caught in the headlights, being held hostage by a crazy person. I know that Cash can have that effect on people. I clear my throat and glance up at Cash.

Mid-sentence he stops, seeing me.

"Hey," he says. Then he turns back to Hooper. "Anyway, man, no one did it better than Gary Oldman in 1992."

I roll my eyes. He's talking about *Dracula*. Poor Hooper.

"This was just the only costume I could find," Hooper says softly with a nervous smile, much like someone who wants to be rescued from a hostage situation.

I chuckle to myself and take a drink of my vodka tonic that I left with Cash. Noelle takes her beer out of Hooper's hand and takes a sip, seemingly none the wiser to the awkward interaction between our two dates.

I would feel bad for Cash, but he brings it on himself.

I want to tell him that not everyone lives Halloween every day of the year like him.

Like *us*.

The thought makes my breath hitch in my chest. I recover quickly.

"What are you guys talking about?" I ask, even though I know. It's just an effort to save Hooper from Cash's hyper-fixation with his costume.

"Just vampire movies," Cash says.

Hooper nods and takes a sip of his drink, entirely uninterested in the topic.

"Anyone want to dance?" Noelle asks.

Hooper looks away, like maybe she won't ask him if he doesn't make eye contact.

"I think your girl wants to dance, man," Cash says.

But the way he says it isn't obtuse. He realizes what he's doing, poking at the guy. I remain silent, eager to see how Hooper reacts. Cash is a fair sight bigger than him and Hooper is, like most sane people are, intimidated slightly by Cash. I don't bother to dispel any scary thoughts he has about the guy. I'm annoyed with Hooper for the way he's treating Noelle.

Hooper looks at Cash and then at Noelle.

"Sure," Hooper says, placing his beer on the table next to us. He takes Noelle's and places it next to his. Then he takes her hand and takes her out on the dance floor.

Cash looks over at me.

"That guy's weird," he says.

"I think they're in a fight," I say.

"Who dresses up as Dracula and doesn't like vampire movies?" he asks, taking a sip of his beer.

"Only a psychopath, I guess," I say, looking up at him, a teasing note in my voice.

"Clearly," Cash says with a grin. Then he looks down at me and there's something in his eyes. Something unsaid. And it's like we look at each other for just a little bit too long. Finally, Cash speaks, and his voice is husky. "You wanna dance?" he asks.

I'm taken aback by the question. I've never been a big dancer. Not ever in my life. In high school, I skipped the prom three times. Noelle begged me to go, over and over again, but I couldn't think of anything more mortifying than dancing in front of my peers.

"I don't really dance," I say.

"Come on," Cash urges.

The song is fast, people are filling the dance floor. My heart beats faster in my chest. As much as I hate looking like a fool, I want to be close to Cash more.

"Okay," I say with a nervous smile.

He takes my drink and sets it on the table next to

our friends'. He takes my hand and drags me out on the floor. His palm is warm, dry, and it swallows up my little hand. He pulls me to the center, just next to a group of people and we start to dance. At first, I'm self-conscious. Then, just as I'm getting the hang of it and he's cheering me on, the song ends, and it's replaced by something far slower.

I stop, almost breathless and smile at him, sure that we're about to head off the dance floor. But Cash reaches for my hand.

I look at his and take it. He pulls me in. I look into his eyes and place my arms on his shoulders. His hands find my waist and my stomach flip flops.

I look down at our feet. The song—a love song—plays loudly on the speakers. The dancers around us have coupled off, all of them slow dancing like we are.

I look up at Cash, meeting his eyes.

His lips part slightly, as if he's going to say something. But he says nothing, ultimately just smiling down at me.

I like the way his hands feel on my hips. I could stay this way for the rest of the night. Us, swaying to the music, just focused on each other. There's something entirely too intimate about it. Even more than when he almost kissed me in Hobby Hollow.

My heart races.

I want to tell him that I want more than a friendship. That I've known it since the beginning on some level. That we're meant for each other.

I part my mouth to speak. To tell him my truth, finally.

But just as I'm about to, I feel a sharp tap on my shoulder and spin.

Noelle. Frantic. Eyes wide.

"Blair," she says.

I break my hold on Cash, and he lets go of me.

"She's here," she says.

I search her face, wondering who she means for the briefest of moments. For a second, I'm lost in a haze of the moment I just shared with Cash. But it occurs to me almost instantly who she's talking about.

Jenna.

And I spin, searching the room. Noelle points to the far side of the dance floor and I spot her.

She's wearing a black dress with a plunging neckline. She looks like she stepped out of a goth music video. She's gorgeous.

She spots Noelle almost instantly. I see it on her face. She steps across the dance floor, cutting through the couples swaying to the slow song that Cash and I were lost in until a moment ago.

I glance at Cash, but his eyes are trained on Jenna. I look back at her as she moves closer. There's something almost ethereal about her.

It's then that I feel a series of vibrations from my purse. The indicator that I have an e-mail waiting for me. I fish it out, and glance at Noelle.

She looks terrified. I reach out a hand for her.

Instead of reaching back, she stares forward, transfixed by the sight of Jenna coming toward us. I take her hand anyway, and without looking over at me, she squeezes it. I squeeze back.

"There you are," Jenna says to Noelle as she saunters up.

Noelle seems to relax slightly.

"Hey," she says to Jenna.

"I thought I'd surprise you," Jenna says. "I got a ticket."

She smiles broadly. Noelle echoes the expression, but the grin doesn't reach her eyes.

Jenna turns her attention to me when Noelle doesn't speak.

"Oh, hi," Jenna says, as if greeting me was only an afterthought. Like she had to lower herself down to my level to even say *hello*.

The jealousy isn't lost on me and there's a part of my mind that's telling me it isn't good to get on Jenna's bad side. But I don't care. My main priority is Noelle and making sure she's safe. And it seems like if Jenna's here, that's one more obstacle between me and Cash keeping Noelle that way.

I glance over at Cash, who has his eyes locked on Jenna. I look back at her, giving her a once over, wondering if she might have a weapon on her. But the dress is skin tight. And her clutch is tiny. If she does, I don't know where she'd be keeping it.

Still, I'm suspicious of her and don't want to let her

and Noelle out of my sight. But judging by the way Noelle is hanging back at my side, I'm not sure she *wants* to be out of my sight.

"Hello," I say to Jenna. I try to keep my voice even, free from a tone of accusation. It could only make the situation worse at this point. She's here and we have to deal with it.

"Could I steal my cousin for a moment?" she asks me, though it's clearly not a question.

She reaches for Noelle and takes her hand.

"Noelle," I start to prevent her from going.

"It's okay," she tells me, looking over her shoulder as Jenna drags her away.

I watch as they part the crowd and then are swallowed by it. I start to take a step in their direction, but Cash's hand holds me back.

"Blair, it's alright," Cash says.

I look up at him.

"It's okay," he says. "I can see them," he adds.

I breathe a sigh of relief. His extreme height proves an advantage once more. I curse myself for being so short. I wish *my* eyes were on the situation, but I trust Cash.

I reach into my purse for my phone, remembering the feeling of vibration letting me know I had an e-mail. There's really only one e-mail I'm waiting for and when I pull my phone out and unlock it, I'm not disappointed.

"Cash," I say. "Look."

I hand him my phone and he reads the e-mail I just read.

The e-mail is from Jonah, of course. The contents tell me that the police are zeroing in on someone, but he's not sure who.

"So, they think Peter might have had something to do with the murders?" Cash asked, furrowing his brow.

"I guess so," I say.

"That just doesn't feel right," Cash says, handing my phone back to me.

"I know what you mean," I say.

And I do.

Something about that just doesn't feel like the truth. I think about what my dad said about Peter and his feelings for Jenna. I trust my dad's judgment.

But, then again, wouldn't a psychopath be able to fool even the most discerning of us?

The whole thing is enough to make my head spin.

I glance over in the direction where Noelle disappeared with Jenna. And then I glance back to where Hooper stands.

But when I look, he's not there.

He's probably looking for her.

"I'm going to go find Noelle," I tell Cash.

"I'll come with you," he says.

And he leads the way through the thick crowd on the dance floor.

CHAPTER TWENTY-SEVEN

BODIES MOVE on either side of us, crowding me to the degree that I almost lose hold of Cash's hand at one point. It causes a little swell of panic in my chest, even though the auditorium isn't that big. I don't want to be stuck in the middle of a crowd. That's never good.

Cash pulls me through to the other side of the auditorium, off the dance floor and over to another area with lots of tables and chairs. I look around, not immediately seeing Noelle or Jenna. For a brief moment, I feel dread. A sinking feeling in my gut takes only seconds to take hold. I whip around and then I spot them.

The two of them are off to the side in a corner. Jenna is saying something to Noelle. Noelle looks to be arguing with her. Whatever Jenna's saying, Noelle wants none of it. Jenna reaches for her as she tries to break away from the conversation.

Noelle spins back to look at Jenna. She jerks her arm out of her cousin's grip. It's almost symbolic, I think as I watch. I feel a surge of pride for Noelle, thinking that she's finally standing up to Jenna. That this could be the beginning of a new era for Noelle. One in which she actually speaks up for herself.

Noelle spins, a horrible look on her face. She looks like a sheet, like whatever Jenna just said to her was horrible. She doesn't even spot me as she marches toward me. I step in front of her and reach out a hand for her shoulder.

"Hey," I say.

Noelle almost jumps out of her skin when I reach for her.

"Hey, I'm sorry!" I tell her.

She looks up at me and then over at Cash.

"Where's Hooper?" she asks.

Apparently, whatever Jenna said to her really spooked her.

"I'm not sure," I tell her honestly.

I look around the room, hoping that I'll spot him. But I don't see him right away. I look back to where Jenna was in the corner, but she's gone now. Almost like a real vampire—here one moment then flitted back into the shadows the next.

I look back at Noelle. Her eyes search the crowd, obviously looking for Hooper. I glance at Cash, and he starts looking around.

"I think he's over at the bar," he tells Noelle.

And without another word to me, she heads out across the dance floor.

"Noelle!" I shout after her, but she doesn't turn around. She's on a mission.

"What the hell do you think that was about?" Cash asks, stepping up beside me. He looks down at me.

"I have no idea," I tell him.

Concern furrows his brow. He glances out into the crowd, looking for Noelle. I watch as his eyes dart around the room. Even with his height, he doesn't find her.

"Do you think we should follow her?" I ask.

Cash seems to think about it. He grabs my hand.

And then he leads me, walking around the dance floor, looking for Noelle.

CHAPTER TWENTY-EIGHT

CASH'S large form parts groups of people ahead of us with ease. Everyone glances as we go by, not at me, but at him. His figure is imposing, an unspoken threat to anyone who might think about messing with him. And tonight, I'm grateful for that. Something feels off.

Like something bad is going to happen and I'm not sure what.

The fact that Jenna is here makes me uneasy.

"Hey!" I shout from behind Cash.

He spins and looks at me, having to pull his attention from the room around us.

"I think if you see Jenna, we need to go talk to her," I say loudly.

Cash takes a deep breath, almost like he's thinking of arguing with me. He's eager to find Noelle, probably because he's just as worried about her as I am. But the same thought occurs to him that did to me. The person that poses her the biggest threat is Jenna. Finding her would accomplish three things: keeping Noelle safe, finding out why Jenna came here tonight, and what she said to Noelle.

This seems to dawn on Cash, and he nods silently at me.

The two of us look around at the tables surrounding us. There are groups of teachers, sipping cocktails and talking over the music. All of them—or at least most—are dressed in costume. There's an air of joviality about the night that seems to have grown from the time that we initially got here.

There's something unsettling about it.

Like Cash and I are the only ones that realize the evening could turn sour suddenly.

Like none of the murders have happened.

And two people directly involved are here tonight.

The thoughts are almost overwhelming and nearly send me into a panic. Of everything I've ended up in the middle of because of Cash, this is the most dangerous.

This time it feels like we're playing with fire.

And everything around us is doused in gasoline.

I swallow, realizing my throat is dry, but I force myself to keep looking for Jenna. She's not over here, though.

"Come on," I say to Cash, taking the lead now.

I can't be worried about what might happen. It will

paralyze me, and I won't be able to do anything to keep Noelle safe. I need to find Jenna. And I can't be afraid.

I glance back to see if he's following me and we walk around the dance floor, looking for her, but to no avail. We come up empty handed at the end of our long, circular trek.

But then, just as we're making our complete circle, I see her blonde head of hair duck out of the auditorium and into the orange and purple hallway. She's leaving.

"There she is!" I shout and point.

I take off before Cash can keep up with me.

"Blair, wait!" I hear him behind me, but there's no time to lose.

I dart into the hallway just in time to see Jenna take a turn into the girl's bathroom. And I jog over and head inside without Cash. Slowing down, I try to make it seem like I'm not chasing her as I come around the corner and enter the restroom. Jenna is at the counter, grabbing a paper towel to dab at her face.

She catches sight of me in the mirror.

"Hello, Jenna," I say, doing my best to sound confident, like she doesn't scare me.

But there's something in her expression that I've never seen there.

A vulnerability and concern she's not known for.

If I didn't know better, I'd swear the tears were real.

"What?" She snaps, sounding frustrated. Her voice quavers.

"Are you okay?" I ask, stepping forward.

"I'm fine," she says. "But Noelle isn't."

"What's that supposed to mean?" I ask, suddenly unnerved and defensive.

"That fucking boyfriend of hers," she says. "He's an asshole. And I tried to tell her that. She wouldn't believe me. Stormed off. Of course, that's how women always are to each other. Always believe their man and not the woman telling on him. Even when it's family," she says, inhaling sharply after the last sentence the way you only can after crying for a long time.

"What?" I ask, not understanding.

"He's been all over me. Texting. Emailing my old high school email address. I didn't even know until last night when I logged back in just to see what was in there," she says.

"What was he telling you? Stay away from Noelle?" I ask, crossing my arms and growing exasperated with Jenna's poor me schtick.

She laughs bitterly.

"You're so stupid, Blair," she says. "He wrote to me *for years*. All the time I was in prison. *Begging* me to answer him. He was in love with me. Obsessed. Just like the rest of them. But apparently, he didn't grow out of it," she says.

I hesitate, silenced.

"W-what?" I manage.

Jenna shakes her head, regaining her mean girl composure.

"He's *still in love with me*. What do you not understand? He doesn't want to be with her. He wants to be with me, Blair."

A sense of horror washes over me.

Hooper is in love with Noelle. Madly.

He always has been.

What the hell is she talking about?

"I'll show you the emails if you don't believe me," she says. And then she grabs her phone out of her purse, navigates to the information she's looking for and shoves it in my face.

I read.

I've waited so long for you to get out of there. You know I've always loved you, worshipped you. I'll leave her in a heartbeat if you say the word.

I feel my stomach turn and my eyes glaze as I read the rest. It all melts together and my heart races, my breathing picks up.

Jenna laughs.

"I tried to tell her, but of course she didn't believe me. Maybe I should send her a screenshot," she remarks, seemingly annoyed rather than devastated for Noelle.

"How many of those are there?" I ask.

"Thousands," she says, pulling the phone back for a second, then flipping it around where I can see her scrolling through all the emails. She's right. There are thousands. Page after page after page. And then she stops.

And I see something that stops my heart.

Hooper's email address.

mrdracula@yahoo.com

I SPIN without saying another word to Jenna and race out of the bathroom, back into the hallway where I run smack into Cash's chest.

"Whoa, are you okay?" He pushes me back, gently squeezing my upper arms.

I'm panting, out of breath, my body trying to let panic take over.

"We need to find Noelle now," I say. "He's here."

"Who's here?" Cash asks, his eyes searching my face for some indication of what I'm talking about.

"Him. Hooper," I say.

Cash looks confused, trying to figure out what I'm telling him.

And then I manage to get it all out.

"He's been emailing Jenna. For years. Telling her he's in love with her and wants to be with her and will leave Noelle in a heartbeat for her. And it's him. He's *him*," I say.

"He's who? Who, Blair?" Cash looks intensely into my eyes.

"Hooper is the guy from my dad's book. The vampire that told him about the people he'd killed. That was him. Writing to my dad. The mrdracula email address. That's the email address he'd been sending those notes to Jenna with. It's him."

Realization seems to settle over Cash's face.

And then there's a piercing scream from the auditorium.

CHAPTER TWENTY-NINE

I RACE INTO THE AUDITORIUM, not waiting for Cash. The music comes to a halt and all anyone can hear is the continued scream. Then suddenly, it ends. And the crowd parts, people scattering off the dance floor.

And in the center, to my horror, is my best friend on her tip toes, clutching Hooper's arm as he holds a knife to her throat.

Cash rushes up behind me and bumps into me. He grabs my arm to steady me.

There's a part of me that's so filled with rage at the sight that I want to rush out onto that dance floor and kill him myself. How *dare* he?

What a fucking little creep! And now Noelle might die because of all this?

People already *have* died, I realize.

A chill descends on me.

It's him.

He's the killer.

"Shut up!" he shouts at Noelle. "Just *shut up!*" He presses the knife into the skin of her throat, and I fight the visceral urge to rush to her. Cash clamps his hand on my upper arm, intent on not letting me go anywhere.

I look over at him, not for reassurance.

And I can tell by the look on his face he can read what I'm feeling. He's angry, too.

"I never would have thought he had it in him," he mutters to himself. Almost like he's infuriated with himself for not picking up on some invisible sign. But neither of us did.

Hooper was good to Noelle.

And then it dawns on me that the reason he was so good to her was probably because he was trying to position himself to get close to Jenna. He was using Noelle. The thought turns my stomach.

All of that for *this?*

It's maddening.

"Where are you, Jenna?!" Hooper shouts.

The scene would be comical. This man dressed as Dracula, holding someone hostage, a bit of Halloween performance art meant to entertain. But that's not what's happening. Instead, it has a different vibe. Horrific and made worse by the atmosphere. Like the party atmosphere has been flipped on its ear, replaced by terror and suffering.

"What the *fuck* are you doing?" Jenna asks, coming forward from the crowd. "Let her go!"

"I can't do that. You know that. It has to be finished," Hooper says, almost desperate. Like there's a part of him that realizes what all of this means for him.

"Let her go," Jenna says evenly.

Before I can think it through or stop myself, the words are out of my mouth, spoken loudly over the crowd.

"Take me instead," I say, stepping forward and worming out of Cash's grip.

He grabs me, trying to jerk me back, but I rush forward and hit my knees.

"Let her go. Take me," I insist.

Hooper looks down at me, shocked.

But then he looks at Jenna, seeming to consider this. I glance at her, horror on her face. She realizes the implications.

"Blair!" Cash shouts from the edge of the dance floor.

I can't look at him. Not now.

"It has to be her," Hooper says under his breath to me.

"No, it doesn't," I say. "It can be me."

I make eye contact with Noelle, tears clinging to the waterlines of her eyes. I have to look away, focus back on Hooper.

"I'm the one you want," I say. "I know who you are, Mr. D."

I pray that it gets through to him.

I go on.

"You can use me to get out of here tonight," I say. "Don't put Noelle in the middle of this. She doesn't deserve that. You can use me."

Hooper seems to think about this.

"If you ever loved her, take me," I beg.

I look at Noelle, trying to communicate silently with my best friend. And it seems to work. I want her to know that I love her. That I always have. I always will, no matter what happens tonight.

But I can't look backwards. I can't look at Cash.

Because if I do, I might not go through with this.

And just then, in a snap, Hooper shoves Noelle away and grabs me by the neck and places me in the position Noelle just occupied.

Then a word—a shout—a single sound breaks over the crowd.

It's my name. Normally something that wouldn't evoke such a feeling in me, but this time it does. And I look at the person who shouted it.

Cash.

Pure terror on his face.

I told myself not to look at him. But it's too late.

As soon as I do, I know exactly how much I have to lose.

CHAPTER THIRTY

I SAY NOTHING. I just stare at Cash, locking eyes with him, trying to tell him the same thing I told Noelle without a single word. And I could swear that he's telling me the same thing and more.

If I'm going to die, I want it to be right now, looking right at him because it's the only thing that feels even remotely safe to me anymore. I think that maybe if I stare into his eyes, I'll forget what's really happening right now. But then I feel the pinch of Hooper's knife at my throat.

"Stay back!" Hooper booms at Cash.

Cash's face is filled with rage, a vein sticking out on his forehead.

"POLICE!" a voice shouts from the hallway and suddenly more than ten armed officers have their guns trained on me and Hooper.

I close my eyes.

He shouts at them, daring them to make a move.

They shout back, telling him to let me go.

I open my eyes and the din around me becomes a dull fuzz in my ears. I look at Cash and he stares at me, pain on his face.

And then suddenly, I feel like I've been hit by a semi-truck. The sheer force of the bullet in my arm is enough to spin me as Hooper tosses me out of his way, my purpose served. And then I hit the ground, the wind knocked out of me. I yell from the pain. There's another gunshot. Then another.

But before a fourth, Cash is at my side, pressing down on the wound in my arm.

"Blair, you're okay," he says. "You're okay."

But I'm not sure he's saying it so much for my benefit as his. I feel dizzy and faint. Shock seems to be taking over and the pain lessens. I can't even feel it now. I just stare at him, his words getting dull in my ears.

I don't know how long it takes and I'm not sure exactly how it happens, but a couple of EMTs descend on me and Cash is forced to move. I want to beg him to stay, but I can't manage the words.

And then, before my eyes can find him again, I pass out.

CHAPTER THIRTY-ONE

I WAKE to the sound of a consistent beep. It's almost comforting and instantly recognizable. The sound of a hospital. A steady monitoring of normal bodily functions. The second thing that occurs to me is that my hand is warm. And the third thing is that my shoulder hurts like a bitch.

"Fuck," I groan, my mouth dry.

And then the warm on my hand squeezes it and I open my eyes.

It's Cash, his hands wrapped around mine.

He breathes a sigh of relief that he tries to conceal by clearing his throat.

"They said you'd be waking up anytime," he says.

"What time is it?" I ask, looking out the window of the hospital room. It's dark.

"About midnight," he says.

"Did I get shot?" I ask, going slowly back over the events that led me here.

Cash chuckles softly.

"Yeah, you got shot."

"Jeeeee-sus Christ," I groan. "It hurts."

"You're probably due for some pain medication," he says and presses the call button on the remote in the bed beside me.

"What happened?" I ask. "All I remember is looking at you and..." I trail off, remembering suddenly the feeling I had as I stared at Cash. The thought that I could lose everything. I could lose *him*.

"Hooper shoved you at just the right time and you took a bullet meant for him. He made a break for it. The cops shot at him, missed, and then grazed him with a bullet that made him drop the knife and stopped him long enough for them to arrest him."

"Did they charge him with the murders?" I ask, trying to sit up but laying back down immediately after trying to put weight on my arm. It's too much.

"I don't know. I came straight here with you," he says. "All I cared about was you."

He stares at me, a vulnerability in his eyes.

He swallows hard, and looks down, still holding my hand.

"I know it's only been a couple of hours," he says, looking up at me with a nervous smile. "But I've had some time to think. Enough time. And there's something I need to tell you, Blair. Whether it works out for me or not," he says.

The beeping from the machine beside me begins to speed up, betraying me, but I don't care.

"I have no idea how you feel. I'm not good at this sort of thing, and I'm not exactly the best at letting people into my life or my heart. But you were like this painless splinter that just slipped under my skin and now you're just part of my life. And tonight, I realized you're part of me, too. Because when I thought you could be gone—" his voice cracks and he clears his throat. "For those terrible minutes, I knew exactly what I stood to lose if something happened to you. And it made me not want to go another terrible minute without you knowing how I feel about you," he says, then pauses.

My heart races.

The machine beeps faster.

"Blair," he says my name and smiles, then rubs the back of my hand with his thumb. "I'm in love with you. And I have been for a while. I knew it fast. Faster than I ever thought I could with anyone. But I knew it deep down in my soul the same way I know who I am. That first time I met you, I knew that whatever happened, I just wanted to be next to you. For as long as you'd let me. And I guess I'm just telling you this because I want to be next to you all the time. Forever. And I hope you'll let me," he says. And then he sighs quickly, like he realizes what's on the line. That he could lose our friendship. "I love you, Blair."

"How are you, Miss Graves?" A nurse appears in the doorway and brushes past Cash.

I'm dumbfounded, unsure of what to say to her. She checks the machine.

"Your heart rate is a little elevated, and I just wanted to check on you."

"Uh, I'm fine," I say. "Just a little excited."

She glances at Cash, my hand in his.

"Oh," she says quietly. She glances back at me as if to ask if it has to do with him and I just smile. She makes quick work of checking my vitals and then disappears out into the hallway, closing the door behind herself, but not before she looks back at Cash. "Don't get her *too* excited."

I laugh, but it hurts.

"Fuck," I murmur. And then I look back at Cash and squeeze his hand. "I love you, too. And I want you to stay right here as long as you want to."

Cash smiles and rubs the back of my hand. He squeezes it lightly and then brings it up to his lips and presses a kiss on the back of my hand firmly.

THEY LET me go the next day.

Cash helps me up into the truck when he picks me up after they wheel me out onto the sidewalk. His hands find my waist and he lifts me effortlessly and shuts the door behind me. We drive wordlessly back to the Solomon House, and he helps me out.

Inside, he gets a place ready for me on the couch, complete with blankets, an RC on the end table, and the remotes within reach. And then he walks me over and sits down with me.

"I thought you might want to watch some *Real Housewives of* Whatever Place," he says.

I smile at him, a little tired from the pain pills, but in good spirits. And the two of us spend the day like that. Me snuggling up next to him. Him planting kisses on my head periodically, like he can't believe I'm okay. Like he's grateful.

I get to talk to Noelle and make sure she's okay, and she refuses to talk about anything other than how I'm doing, insisting that she'll come over just as soon as I'm ready. I thank her and make plans to see her tomorrow.

Before I know it, the ten o'clock news is on and it's night again.

And Hooper's face pops up on screen as the lead story. I sit up straight onto the edge of my seat. Cash leans forward, too and turns up the volume.

"Last night, terror dominated a local high school's Halloween gathering for its teachers," the anchor says. It's the same young blonde woman that first reported on all of this. "Former Moore High School teacher Mr. Hooper has been arrested after holding his girlfriend and one of the other guests at knifepoint before police were alerted and arrived on the scene. One woman was shot in the altercation with police, but she is already home from the hospital and doing well according to the Moore Police Department. Hooper faces various charges from the incident last night, but the most concerning might be potential murder charges he could face from recent vampire-like killings connected to the release of Jenna Prescott who attempted to murder her step-father with the help of a group of friends who played a vampire role-playing game."

I sit there, absorbing it.

After the story is over, Cash turns the volume down again and reaches his arm around me, tugging me back to his side. The warmth of his body is welcome. I relax against him.

"I gave the cops all the info I could last night. Jenna showed them the e-mails. I think she was eager to lift the suspicion off herself. Noelle was pretty upset about everything, but she told me she was okay. Jenna stayed with her last night. I think she's in shock. Who wouldn't be?" Cash asks.

"Don't turn out to be a murderer," I say. "I don't think I can handle that on top of everything else." I look at him.

"Oh, don't worry," he says. "The things you'll find out about me and my family will be way more complicated than murder," he says with a smirk.

"Can't be worse than any of this," I say, gesturing at the television.

"You'd be surprised," Cash teases.

Or maybe he's not teasing. Maybe he does have complicated secrets and relationships. But I really don't care how complicated it gets. I just want *this*.

He presses his forehead to mine, cupping his hand gently on the back of my neck. I grab his wrist and lean forward, closing my eyes.

I feel his breath fanning across my throat and chest, warm and smelling vaguely like mint. He pulls back slightly, and I open my eyes. His, half-closed, look down at me. He strokes the side of my face with his thumb.

And then he leans in and presses his mouth to mine, a gentle, warm kiss. He pulls me closer, conscious of my injured arm and doing his best not to hurt me. But to hell with that. I don't care. The kiss turns passionate, needful and something deep inside me responds to his touch. Finally, I pull away, breathless.

"Take me upstairs," I whisper.

He presses his forehead to mine for a moment, then lifts me from the couch and carries me out of the living room, up the stairs and into my bedroom. He sits me on the bed softly and switches on the soft light of the lamp.

"You sure you want that on?" I tease.

He looks at me with grave seriousness on his face, no room for a joke.

"I want to see you," he says, sitting down on the bed next to me.

Cash reaches for my face and kisses me, soft and sensual nudging me closer to the point where I'm going to beg him for more. I reach for the hem of his shirt and pull it up. He helps me, shedding the garment onto the floor and I press my good hand to his chest. His skin is hot, almost fevered, and I can feel his heart beating fast in his chest.

Now it's my turn, it seems. Cash slowly reaches for my shirt, gently getting it over my arm and effortlessly off and onto the floor.

And when the cold air of the room hits my skin, it dawns on me that I'm not wearing anything under it. I haven't been since we left the hospital. And I suddenly feel exposed. I reach to cover myself, but he stops my hand.

"No," he breathes. His voice is husky, gruff.

And he takes me in.

I can't take it anymore and I reach for his belt. He reaches for the buttons of my jeans. In a flurry of activity, the clothes are gone and Cash lays me down on my bed gently. He leans over me, supporting himself with one arm, the other running across my skin, his eyes reverent. Like this is a religious experience. And it might be.

"This is your last chance," he whispers, then kisses my neck. He pulls back and looks into my eyes.

"Because I think if go any further, I'm never going to be able to let you go."

I press a kiss to his mouth, grabbing his jaw with my good hand. Then I pull away.

I reach up to feel his heart beating in his chest.

"Fuck," he says, his eyes on mine. "I fucking love you, Blair."

"I fucking love you, too, Cash," I whisper.

CHAPTER THIRTY-TWO

WHEN I WAKE UP, this time he's still in the bed with me.

"Good morning," he says sleepily, playing with my hair, my head on his chest. Our legs are tangled up in each other and the blankets. I'm not sure that our bodies have gone a second without touching since we got in bed last night.

"Morning," I say.

And then a wave of pain hits me, my bad arm aching mercilessly. I groan and grit my teeth.

"Pain pills," I say through gritted teeth.

Cash stretches his long arm toward the nightstand and grabs them, along with a glass of water.

"Went down and got these earlier. I knew you'd probably need them," he says, helping me sit up to take the pills and a drink. "How do you feel?" he asks.

"It hurts," I say. "Bad," I add with a laugh that ultimately makes me groan because of how much it irritates my arm. I look over at him. He's gorgeous. And the concern on his face is cute. I smirk back at him. "But you're not asking about my arm, are you?"

He laughs nervously, then reaches to brush hair out of my face.

"Well, I was asking about your arm...and you, you know. You and me," he says, clearing his throat.

"I'm good," I say. "Very good."

"Me, too," he says with a smile.

He places a kiss on my forehead.

"I want to stay right here with you forever," I say softly.

Cash leans in and kisses me on the mouth so softly and tenderly that it hurts my heart from how nice it is.

"Okay," he says, pulling me close to him, laying back down in the bed and I follow his lead. "Let's stay here."

He plays with my hair and before long, the pain has lessened and I fall asleep again.

IN THE EVENING, Noelle comes over and Cash orders takeout food for all of us. He lets us have the couch after dinner and Noelle gets me up to speed on everything.

"I just can't believe it," she says. "But you know, I probably should have seen something like this coming? Maybe him still being in love with Jenna. But not the rest. Not the murders. Who the hell would have pinned Hooper for a murderer?"

"I certainly didn't," Cash chimes in. "He's just such a mild-mannered guy."

"It's always the quiet ones," I add. "Isn't that what they say, anyway?"

"I guess so," Noelle says. "I just feel so disappointed in myself that I didn't—I don't know—pick up on any of this, I guess."

Cash gets Noelle a glass of wine and more water for me in a stainless-steel tumbler. I smile up at him when he hands it to me and he bends down to kiss me, smiles, then heads back into the kitchen.

Noelle clocks it instantly.

Her eyes widen and she gets a knowing look on her face.

"Oh my God," she whispers as he leaves the room. "Is it official? Are you a thing?"

"Kind of, yeah," I say, catching Cash looking back and winking at me. I smile at Noelle.

"Blair," she says. "Did you guys?" She shakes her head. "Surely not, your arm. I forgot about your arm. God," she says.

I say nothing, but a shit-eating grin creeps up at the corners of my mouth.

"Oh, my *God*. How was it?" She whispers conspiratorially.

"It was great," I say, trying to remain somewhat mysterious.

"Details," she says.

"I can't do that here," I say with a laugh. "Maybe when he goes home."

"I bet he's not going anywhere," Noelle says with a laugh.

We talk for a few more hours and Cash gives us some room but doesn't ignore us. Finally, Noelle gets up to leave and I walk her to the door. She wraps me in a tight embrace, avoiding my injured shoulder.

"Hold on to him, Blair," she says. "I think this one is different."

"We'll see," I say. Even though, deep down, I think she's right.

Cash comes to give her a hug, too, and we all say goodbye.

Just as I shut the door, I hear my phone ringing in the other room. I look at Cash, wondering who it is. He's usually the only person besides Noelle that calls me.

I rush back into the living room and grab my phone, face down, on the couch.

Blake

I stare at his name for a moment, unsure of exactly what I'm seeing. I worry briefly that I might be hallucinating.

I slide my finger across the screen to answer.

"Hello?" I say.

"Blair!" Blake says, breathless, terrified.

"What's going on?"

"You have to come, now!" he whispers. Almost like he's trying to keep someone from hearing him.

"Come where? Where are you?" My voice goes up in pitch. Suddenly Cash looks concerned, standing across the room from me.

"—Jersey. I'm in the—" the line goes in and out. I can't make out the rest of what he says. "—barren."

"Where are you?" I shout into the phone.

"I have to go. Please come," he says. "Dad was right."

And then he hangs up the phone and I'm left staring at mine.

"Who was it?" Cash asks.

"Blake," I say. "Umm, I think he might be in trouble. Like he might need me to go to him."

"What's going on? Where is he?"

"He said something about Jersey. That he's in something. He mentioned the word *barren*. I don't know. A field or something?"

"Barren," Cash repeats. "Did he say anything else?"

"Yeah," I say, and a chill washes over me. "He said 'Dad was right.'"

Cash's face falls.

"I know where he is," he says. "We gotta go."

"Where are we going?" I ask, suddenly feeling frantic.

"New Jersey," Cash says. "The Pine Barrens."

"How do you know that? What does that mean?"

"Your dad went to New Jersey to look for something very specific. And if Blake is in Jersey and he thinks your dad was right, there's only one place he could be. And that's the Pine Barrens."

"What's in the Pine Barrens? What the hell was my dad looking for?"

Cash hesitates for a moment. Then he speaks.

"The Jersey Devil."

JOIN MY NEWSLETTER

Sign up now and get a free horror novella, The Body Snatchers. You'll also get updates, freebies, news about me and my dogs, plus book discounts and sales!

Sign up here:

https://BookHip.com/PZGBMZT

ALSO BY MARNIE VINGE

SHOP NOW

www.marniewritesthrillers.com

Psychological Thrillers

The Getaway

Swingers

For Rosie

I Remember Everything

Cold Blood

Women's Thrillers

The Way It Ends

What We Did That Night

Manspreader

The Blair Graves Files

The Haunting of Solomon House

The Holloway Hoax

The Vampire's Game

One Night in September

Short Horror Collections

Thicker Than Water

In Sheep's Clothing

The Reunion

Romance

Gunshy

www.ingramcontent.com/pod-product-compliance
Lightning Source LLC
Chambersburg PA
CBHW021512240626
47154CB00002B/596